THE MYSTERIOUS CURE

and Other Stories
of Pshrinks Anonymous

By J. O. Jeppson

THE MYSTERIOUS CURE

and Other Stories
of Pshrinks Anonymous

J. O. JEPPSON

DOUBLEDAY & COMPANY, INC.

GARDEN CITY, NEW YORK

1985

ACKNOWLEDGMENTS

Introduction by Isaac Asimov copyright © 1985 by Nightfall, Inc.

"The Mysterious Cure" copyright © 1982 by Davis Publications, Inc. Originally appeared in *Isaac Asimov's Science Fiction Magazine*.

"The Hotter Flash" copyright © 1981 by Davis Publications, Inc. Originally appeared in *Isaac Asimov's Science Fiction Magazine*.

"A Million Shades of Green" copyright © 1981 by Davis Publications, Inc. Originally appeared in *Isaac Asimov's Science Fiction Magazine*.

"Seasonal Special" copyright © 1984 by TSR, Inc. Originally appeared in *Amazing Science Fiction Stories*.

"The Beanstalk Analysis" copyright © 1980 by Davis Publications, Inc. Originally appeared in *Isaac Asimov's Science Fiction Magazine*.

"The Horn of Elfland" copyright © 1983 by Davis Publications, Inc. Originally appeared in *Isaac Asimov's Science Fiction Magazine*.

"A Pestilence of Psychoanalysts" copyright © 1980 by Davis Publications, Inc. Originally appeared in *Isaac Asimov's Science Fiction Magazine*.

"Consternation and Empire" copyright © 1981 by Davis Publications, Inc. Originally appeared in *Isaac Asimov's Science Fiction Magazine*.

"The Ultimate Biofeedback Device" copyright © 1983 by Davis Publications, Inc. Originally appeared in *Isaac Asimov's Science Fiction Magazine*.

"The Curious Consultation" copyright © 1982 by Davis Publications, Inc. Originally appeared in *Isaac Asimov's Science Fiction Magazine*.

"The Time-Warp Trauma" copyright © 1981 by Davis Publications, Inc. Originally appeared in *Isaac Asimov's Science Fiction Magazine*.

Library of Congress Cataloging in Publication Data
Jeppson, J. O.
The mysterious cure, and other stories of Pshrinks Anonymous.
1. Science fiction, American. 2. Psychiatrists—Fiction. I. Title.
PS3560.E6M87   1985   813'.54

ISBN: 0-385-19085-9
Library of Congress Catalog Card Number 84-21160
Copyright © 1985 by NIGHTFALL, INC.
All Rights Reserved
Printed in the United States of America

First Edition

CONTENTS

DEDICATION

To the William Alanson White Institute of
Psychoanalysis

INTRODUCTION

BY ISAAC ASIMOV

Although J. O. (Janet) Jeppson is a real Pshrink, and is (I imagine) a tower of strength in her psychiatric office, she is a shrinking violet in the real world. She has a tendency to hide behind the drapes at cocktail parties and when asked to speak in public, she responds with elaborate mumbles.

Her ideal is to remain anonymous and invisible, which is hard, since she is married to me, and I am totally unscrupulous about keeping her in the limelight.

She manages to keep her patients anonymous, to be sure, since she never talks about them, and I believe her when she says that no one in these stories is based on any person, living, dead, or in between. —With one exception.

There is an Interpersonal in each story who, I find from various subtle internal clues, resembles my charming wife. Janet says the Interpersonal is the person she would *like* to be, but since they both have a number of things in common, such as allergies, and difficult but brilliant husbands, the resemblance is clearly total.

People often ask Janet what it's like to be married to a famous, incredibly handsome author, and she always smiles happily and jumps up and down and claps her hands in glee. Later, she says to me, "Isaac, why don't people ask *you* what it's like to be married to a psychiatrist?"

When I start to answer, she interrupts, looking around nervously to see if anyone is listening. It's odd the way

Pshrinks—even those who are not my wife—have a tendency to interrupt incredibly handsome authors who also talk exceedingly well.

Janet says, "Please don't ever tell anybody!"

Since she won't let me give any of the details even if I were asked what it's like to be married to a Pshrink, no one will ever know.

And no one will ever know what it's like to be married to a Pshrink who is also an author. It is my eternal secret both before and after I end up in a padded cell.

THE MYSTERIOUS CURE

and Other Stories
of Pshrinks Anonymous

THE MYSTERIOUS CURE

"How did you do it?" said the Youngest Member of Pshrinks Anonymous, addressing one of the Interpersonals who infested, according to the Oldest Member, the weekly luncheon meetings of the Psychoanalytic Alliance. "How did you manage to cure Mr. ——— in one session?"

"No names!" shouted the Oldest Member, in a bad mood ever since he'd discovered that the main course was to be Logorrheic Liver Lasagna.

The Youngest Member gulped.

"Well, I—" began the Interpersonal.

"Now see here!" said the Oldest Member. "Since I've heard the name, I assume that it's the same patient I did a consultation on after he was discharged from the hospital last year. No one could have cured him in one session."

The O.M. turned to one of his Freudian colleagues, a quiet man who seldom spoke. "I distinctly remember sending that patient to *you* for therapy, not to any Interpersonal."

The quiet Freudian nodded. "Unfortunately the patient left after one session."

The Oldest Member groaned and turned to the Interpersonal. "Then how did he get to you? Are you presuming to claim that he's cured?"

"I didn't know he was permanently cured," said the Interpersonal, stirring Vegetable Vice soup to see what would come up. "It's probably a long story."

"I don't want to hear it. Especially in public."

"Are we public? Isn't one point of these lunches that by keeping ourselves and our patients anonymous, we can discuss issues which may teach us a few things?" said the Interpersonal.

"This patient is no longer anonymous," said the Oldest Member severely. "Our token psychiatric resident here has not yet learned the rules."

"Forgive me," said the Youngest, "but I got excited when I ran into him on the way here, and he seemed so healthy and happy, after being so strangely psychotic in the Intensive Care Unit last year when I was a medical student there. He said he hadn't hallucinated for six months."

"Since his consultation with me?" said the Interpersonal as she fished up a particularly phallic vegetable of undiagnosable species and vintage.

"Yes."

"Flummery," muttered the Oldest Member, who had not been able to find anything in his soup except peas.

"I'd like to hear about the case," said another Pshrink. "I didn't even catch the name, and if I did, I'll keep it to myself."

Several other Pshrinks spoke at once, saying they wanted to hear about quick cures for hallucinations.

"I remember," said the Interpersonal, "that he was quite a loner, with no family to keep tabs on him. The case is really quite odd, I suspect; and perhaps those of us who saw him, however briefly, can put things together and figure out why I did cure him, if I did." She paused and frowned. "Come to think of it, I think I can guess *how* I cured him. It's the *why* I'd like to know more about. And the more I think about it, the cure is not as mysterious as the psychiatric disorder itself. I'd like very much to hear about the encounters other Pshrinks had with him."

As everyone else murmured in agreement, the Oldest Member snorted and tugged at his moustache.

"Careful," said the Interpersonal. "You're spoiling the waxed tips."

"Oh, go ahead and indulge yourself," he said finally. "Tell us the story."

"But it's *our* story, all four of us. Let's begin with the Youngest Member's description of—we'll call him Mr. X—in the ICU."

"Okay," said the Youngest, sitting upright and composing his face, as young doctors learn to do when they are reporting on cases to older and ostensibly wiser colleagues. "Mr. X was admitted to the ICU by his internist, who had diagnosed a dangerous cardiac arrhythmia requiring the implantation of a pacemaker. Mr. X is an elderly male—"

"Elderly my foot!" roared the Oldest Member. "He's not even sixty! He's in early middle age!"

"You must forgive the young," said the Interpersonal. "To them anyone over forty is a geriatrics problem."

"Sorry," said the Youngest, with no visible signs of contrition. "Anyway, Mr. X was, except for his irregular heartbeat, in reasonably good health considering the injuries he had sustained in World War II, as well as the fact that he was—er —in early middle age."

"What were the injuries?" asked the quiet Freudian, who had obviously never asked the patient.

"He'd had a head injury, with some loss of hearing and a small piece of shrapnel buried in his skull. The hearing loss had been correctable with a hearing aid; and since the shrapnel was minute and didn't seem to cause any trouble, no one thought it necessary to remove it."

"Mr. X told me he didn't know of any electroencephalographic abnormalities," said the Interpersonal. "Were there any?"

"None," said the Youngest, "and that was one of the first things the house staff tested when he began to have such peculiar hallucinations. He was on a disabled veteran's partial pension for the head wound and of course the leg that was amputated when a land mine blew up near him; but he'd managed quite well physically until he got a new job, an advancement that produced so much nervous tension he began to have palpitations that eventually became serious."

"Tension? Or arteriosclerosis?" said the Oldest Member, who was still scowling.

"As far as anyone could tell, tension," said the Youngest Member. "They even did a cardiac catheterization but no evidence of structural abnormality or arteriosclerosis could be found. The cardiologists decided that a pacemaker would protect him from any dire results of the arrhythmia."

"Didn't they consider tranquilizers first?" asked an Eclectic.

"Oh, sure. I forgot. Lots of tranquilizers and visits to a few therapists had been tried before he went to the hospital. The heart went on acting up, so the pacemaker went in."

"And that's when he became psychotic?" asked the Oldest Member.

"Yes."

"Right away?" asked the Interpersonal.

"No. That was the odd thing. As you know, it's not uncommon for patients who are hooked up to a lot of machinery while seriously ill to have episodes of depersonalization or even hallucinations—in the Coronary Care Unit, or on renal dialysis, or in the ICU. I guess patients with tubes in every orifice and machinery clicking around them, monitoring everything their bodies are doing, have a right to feel they've lost touch with their own humanness."

"Nicely put," said the Interpersonal, smiling at the Youngest.

"Thanks. Mr. X had been hooked up to cardiac monitors and intravenous equipment and the other paraphernalia, but while in bed he was doing just fine mentally. I paid a lot of attention to him because he was so normal compared to a lot of the other patients. Then came the day he was ready to leave the hospital because the pacemaker was working well, and he got dressed and suddenly began to hallucinate."

"Didn't want to leave, I suppose," said a Pshrink who still worked in hospitals because she was addicted to them.

"I don't know," said the Youngest, looking uncomfortable.

"What were the hallucinations at that time?" asked the Oldest Member, who now had that Avidly Listening Pshrink look on his face.

"He began talking about people who seemed to be inside his head, along with vivid pictures that were like a combination of hieroglyphics and bird tracks marching across in straight lines, blotting out and reappearing in different combinations."

"He *saw* the people?"

"No, he heard them. Or maybe he didn't. It wasn't something he could explain easily. He kept talking about what these people were doing, which kept changing. One of them had a guttural name—I'll say 'Ugh' although that wasn't it—and the other two had pleasant names I can't remember, since they weren't very pronounceable. I'll call them A and B. It seems that Ugh had it in for A and B and kept chasing them, with intent to kill."

"Oedipal hallucinations would bother anyone," said the Oldest Member, with the placidity of one who feels he is on safe ground.

"But it wasn't A or B or what Ugh was going to do to them that bothered Mr. X," said the Youngest. "While he was hallucinating he kept shouting that he couldn't stand the changes. No one knew what he meant until later when he explained it a little to me."

"Why did you let him out of the hospital?" said a Pshrink.

"We didn't. The house staff gave him a sedative and he fell asleep almost standing up. He went on mumbling about A and B in his sleep until we got his clothes off and put him back in bed. He woke up the next day remembering the hallucinations but not experiencing them. He felt great and insisted on signing out of the hospital. Then when he got dressed and was leaving the ward, he began to hallucinate again. That scared him, so he agreed to stay for a psychiatric consultation.

"Days passed, and he didn't hallucinate again, so the psychiatric consultant and the medical staff decided to try discharging him on the condition that he would immediately go to see a psychiatrist. He got dressed and I noticed that he was quite pale. He denied that he was hallucinating, but I'm sure he was."

"You are correct," said the Oldest Member, brushing a crumb of Rationalized Roll off his tweed lapel. "He *was* hallucinating and as soon as he was back in his apartment he called the name he'd been given—mine. I had a cancellation later that afternoon, so I saw him. The hallucinations had stopped, but he was worried. I thought he should go into long-term analysis, and at first he agreed. Since I always try to do at least two consultations before making a definitive referral, we made another appointment for the next day. He canceled it."

"Then that's all you saw of him?" said the Interpersonal.

"No, a week later he came for another consultation, this time saying he wanted a referral. I was too busy to fit him into my schedule permanently, so I sent him to one of my colleagues who is interested in the analytic treatment of psychotics. Although Mr. X didn't seem terribly psychotic, there were the undeniable hallucinations which he said occurred every day for at least a couple of hours. He had not told anyone about them, and apparently even his internist thought that he'd had only a momentary mental aberration while still in the hospital. Mr. X's physical condition was good, the pacemaker working perfectly when it had to, which was seldom."

"Seldom?" asked the Youngest Member. "Why?"

"Because Mr. X's illness had changed his attitude toward his job," said the Oldest Member. "The arrhythmia accordingly quieted down when his psyche did."

"What job?" asked a Pshrink.

"If I remember correctly, he's a top editor of textbooks at some publishing house—"

"Turgid textbooks," said the Interpersonal.

"—and Mr. X said the silliness of the hallucinations somehow made his job seem easier. The ceaseless, changing, and basically boringly banal adventures of A and B pursued by Ugh were enough to make him relax at work. He wanted a referral for therapy only because he was embarrassed by the hallucinations and wanted to get rid of them."

"And I was embarrassed," said the quiet Freudian, a small, thin man, "by Mr. X's failure to come back after only one session, so I didn't call you up [he glanced apologetically at the O.M.] and find out more about his hallucinations. You see, he came only because he'd found my name in his appointment book. He couldn't remember having made the appointment, and he couldn't remember seeing you."

"That's bizarre," said the Oldest Member. "I know that he had neatly circumscribed times when he hallucinated, but he remembered them perfectly well when I saw him."

"He must have had a fugue state," said the quiet Freudian, "complete with total amnesia for the psychosis. I forgot to mention that in addition to finding my name, he found a collection of scribbled sheets of paper upon which he'd also written my name and telephone number. Most of the sheets —which I saw—were covered with undecipherable gibberish in an unknown language."

"Bird tracks and hieroglyphics?" asked the Youngest.

"Something like that. What interested me was that he'd written in the margins, in clear, readable English, critical expressions like 'trite, lousy style, what trash'—the sort of remarks a very angry professional editor might put on a manuscript."

"What happened to the manuscript?" asked the Interpersonal eagerly.

"He handed it to me and asked me to destroy it. I think he believed that if I did so, the hallucinations would not come back. I do not ordinarily pander to neurotic impulses of neurotic patients, much less give in to psychotics, but I found myself walking out into the hall with Mr. X. He watched while I threw the thing into the incinerator. He thanked me and said he didn't need a Pshrink anymore. Then he paid in cash and left. That was last October."

"Early October?" asked an Eclectic.

"I think so. Why do you ask?"

"Because late in October his internist sent him to me for a psychiatric consultation," said the Eclectic.

"Five of us!" said the Oldest Member. "Mr. X actually saw five of us Pshrinks—without remembering the previous episodes of hallucinations?"

"When I saw him," said the Eclectic, "he said he had begun to hallucinate for the first time, and told his internist about it. He knew, of course, that he'd had some sort of psychological upset while in the hospital to get his pacemaker—that was on the records—but he'd forgotten about the other times he'd seen Pshrinks, because I didn't get that history until I listened to the rest of you today."

"Was he frightened?" said the Interpersonal matter-of-factly.

"I thought it was odd that he wasn't. He seemed bored and disgusted with the hallucinations. He said it was like having to read a particularly hackneyed B novel over and over; and he felt ashamed that his own imagination, which he assumed was somehow producing the hallucinations, was so sadly disorganized, banal, and dull. He prided himself, he said, on being a skillful editor and knowing good writing; but he had no control over the story going on in his head. I recommended antipsychotic medication but Mr. X refused and left. I never saw him again."

"But I did," said one of the Adlerians who had not spoken before but had listened to the others with an expression of astonishment. "I knew him slightly at college, and that may have been why he called me—probably not long after he'd seen our esteemed Eclectic here. He said he was having strange hallucinations for two hours every day, couldn't remember having them before, and had decided to ask me what to do about them because he was afraid to tell his internist. I agreed to have a late lunch with him—I didn't want to be his therapist—and we talked about it at length. He seemed perfectly sane, his heart was doing well, he was happy in his job, and he was even becoming more social, which was another reason the hallucinations embarrassed him. I thought that perhaps they were the sort of hypnagogic hallucinations that occur sometimes in normal people when they are sleepy, but I changed my mind when Mr. X began to hallucinate right in my presence, in the restaurant."

"What were the hallucinations?" asked the Interpersonal.

"It sounded as if he were making up a story as he went along, a silly plot about a villain and a hero and a heroine, although I'm not that sure about the sexes and I couldn't make out the setting or the exact ramifications of the plot because he'd keep changing them. The villain did sound like 'Ugh,' and I think Mr. X was hung up on whether or not Ugh should attack a planet with a stolen spaceship with B in it. Or was it A?"

The Oldest Member shoved aside the remains of the lasagna he had been picking at, and said, "Are you telling me that this textbook editor writes or edits science fiction on the sly, or that he did?"

"No," said the Adlerian. "I asked him that. He said he never read fiction if he could help it, except revered old classics, preferably Russian. He disapproved of science fiction and was terribly upset that he seemed to be making up not only SF but *bad* SF in his head."

The Interpersonal giggled.

The Adlerian nodded to her and said, "I gave him your name—he wrote it down—because I thought someone versed in SF might tune into his problems better. He thanked me and we finished lunch."

"With Mr. X hallucinating all through dessert?" said the Oldest Member.

"Yes, but quietly, as if he were faintly amused by it. I was flabbergasted by what happened next. As we walked together out of the restaurant, he suddenly turned to me and said, 'Why, Joe! Haven't seen you in ages! How are you? Have you already had lunch?' "

"Do you mean to say that X had absolutely no memory of calling you, having lunch with you, hallucinating to beat the band?" said the Oldest Member.

"That's right. I gently asked him about the hallucinations and he stared at me as if I were crazy. I pretended to be joking and he walked off, presumably still carrying in his pocket the piece of paper with the referral on it."

"Well," said the Oldest Member to the Interpersonal. "Now it's your turn. You finish this case history or I may get indigestion and sue the club."

"I'll do my best," said the Interpersonal, who had eaten all her portion of liver lasagna because she thought it was good for her. "Mr. X called me sometime in November, I think it was. He said he'd found my name on a prescription blank apparently given him by his old college buddy, whom he had not consulted—as far as he knew. He'd looked me up and found that I'm a Pshrink, so he thought maybe he ought to try it, because he was having embarrassing hallucinations that had first started a week previously."

"Maybe he's lying about these supposed amnesiac episodes," said the Oldest Member.

"I don't think so," said the Interpersonal. "Of course, I didn't know about the other episodes; but he seemed genuinely puzzled about how he had acquired the paper with my name on it; and he was even more puzzled by his hallucinations, which came only at set times, usually right after lunch, and only lasted for two or three hours. In fact, Mr. X could do his own work right through the period of hallucinations if he concentrated hard enough. What disturbed and embarrassed him was that he was becoming—not frightened, but *intrigued* by them."

"What was dull had become intriguing?" said the Eclectic.

"So it seems," said the Interpersonal. "He asked me for an hour right after lunch, which I provided. He came in complaining about various aches and pains—"

"He did?" said the Adlerian. "I've just remembered that before he started to hallucinate in the restaurant, he complained a little about something aching. I think it was his head. Or maybe it was his leg."

"His teeth," said the Oldest Member. "I remember he told me that they bothered him."

"I'm sure it was his head, near the shrapnel wound," said the Eclectic.

"Gee," said the Youngest Member. "I remember now that when he was getting dressed, ready to go home, he did complain a little about some aches—and this was before the hallucinations started."

"There are many neurological conditions leading to hallucinations that have prodromal signs like mysterious pains," said the Eclectic, who had once been a neurologist.

"But it was only when he was strapping on his artificial leg that he began complaining," said the Youngest. "And I don't remember his having a removable dental bridge that he put in before going home. We make a record of everything removable like that."

"He definitely didn't have a removable bridge," said the Interpersonal. "He had a lot of fillings. Old fillings."

"You say that portentously," said the Oldest Member. "Is it supposed to mean something?"

"Old fillings dating from the thirties and forties frequently were put in without the base material that's now used. I've had some of the problems myself . . ."

"Hallucinations, m'dear?"

"Of course not. Toothache—from electrical resonance or whatever it is that bollixes up the teeth and makes them ache because of those damn old fillings that have to come out."

The Oldest Member leaned forward, brows beetling. "Do you have the gall to tell us that you didn't even cure this patient with dubious interpersonal analysis? You just sent him to a dentist?"

"Not exactly. When Mr. X started to describe his hallucinations, as he was having them during the session, they were about Ugh and A and B, just as the rest of you have said, but I found them to be interesting. The characters, whoever they were, seemed fully drawn and their adventures thrilling, even elaborate. As an SF aficionado, I confess that I didn't find them trite at all. I remember thinking I wished I had a tape recorder so I'd be able to remember them later."

"And steal the plot?" asked the Oldest Member.

"Certainly not! At least, I think—I hope—but that's beside the point. While Mr. X was describing the hallucinations, I noticed that he seemed to be in pain that was more severe than the minor complaints he'd had before the hallucinations started. It was as if everything ached horribly—his thigh above the artificial leg, his head near the shrapnel wound, his ear, his teeth, the skin over his pacemaker—not, fortunately, his chest *under* the pacemaker. He said he'd gone to a dentist recently and had been told he ought to have his old fillings replaced, but he was beginning to believe that it wouldn't help because he was falling apart. What really scared him, which he wouldn't talk about at first, was his fear that the pacemaker was responsible for the aches and pains in the rest of his body, as well as what he thought were new symptoms of hallucinations."

"Then how did you cure him?" asked the Oldest Member. "Send him to his dentist? Or is the poor guy minus his pacemaker now?"

"I thought that the pacemaker ought to come out last,

since that was the most essential of all the pieces of metal in or on his body."

"But what's metal got to do with it?" asked a Pshrink.

"I thought there might be electronic complications, if I'm using the word correctly, and I'm probably not," said the Interpersonal. "Depending on the point of view of the examiner, one can say that the nervous system functions chemically—or physiologically—or psychiatrically, or whatever. But from another point of view the nervous system is an electronic marvel which might get upset by too much metal impinging on it in some way."

"Aha!" said the Oldest Member. "You told Mr. X to have the shrapnel removed. It was behaving like a radio receiver."

"Was it? I don't know. I wanted—as any Pshrink would be tempted to do—to investigate the interesting psychodynamics of the hallucinations, but I thought that first he ought to have the aches and pains investigated. In fact, I decided to do a little preliminary investigating myself."

"Trust an Interpersonal to do something un-Pshrinkish."

"Yes. I did the simplest thing first. I asked him to take off his hearing aid."

There was silence in the dim dining room of Pshrinks Anonymous.

"I see you are all struck dumb before my brilliance," said the Interpersonal. "After all, a hearing aid is electronic and it was the most easily removable gadget on Mr. X. He took it off and the hallucinations promptly stopped. When I asked him to put it back on, the hallucinations started again. Then he took off his artificial leg; and presto, no hallucinations. It didn't seem to matter which piece of metal he removed as long as it was something.

"He decided to go without his hearing aid until he saw his dentist. A few days later he called me to say that the new fillings were a great success. He could wear his leg and his hearing aid, and of course the pacemaker and the shrapnel, without being bothered by hallucinations. I tried to interest him in some therapy, because I thought the nature of the hallucinations warranted psychoanalytic investigation, but he refused."

"And since then he's been okay, for six months," said the Youngest. "This explains why Mr. X had the hallucinations only after he got fully dressed—and equipped—when he was ready to leave the hospital. And it must explain why he had them only during the day."

"Any true Pshrink," said the Oldest Member, "would say that if too many bits of metal can hook up electronically so as to bring out the repressed Oedipal problems in such a psychotic manner, then a proper analysis was indicated."

"I believe that, in my Interpersonal way, I've already said that," said the Interpersonal. "Now, however, after hearing that he's been free of hallucinations for six months, I think all of us who've seen him should knuckle down and do some analysis ourselves. Remember that he hallucinated in a very interesting way, at specific times."

"I'm a witness," said the Adlerian, "to the fact that the hallucinations would stop abruptly with resulting total amnesia for the episode, although he was still wearing all the metal."

"He must have been putting you on," said the Oldest Member. "Didn't our Youngest Member say that Mr. X remembered the hallucinations well from one time to the next? He certainly remembered having had them when he came to see me."

"But by the time he saw me," said the quiet Freudian, "he'd forgotten them."

"And when he saw me," said the Eclectic, "he remembered having had days of hallucinations—but he didn't remember the previous episode."

"He'd hallucinate regularly for days, and then start all over again as if from scratch. Does that remind anyone of anything?" asked the Interpersonal.

"I suppose you have something weird in mind?" said the Oldest Member with a bit of a leer.

"Perhaps I have not mentioned it here," said the Interpersonal, "but many writers nowadays have sold their souls to machines which function very much like this poor patient's psychosis."

"Oh come now," said the Oldest Member. "We're not that far into the science fiction world of the future."

"I'm afraid we are," said the Interpersonal. "A word processor can be used to rewrite and rewrite endlessly, the unwanted words disappearing miraculously, the day's work stored on floppy discs which the computer uses to spew the whole thing out into the printer when that version is produced. The writer of Ugh versus A and B seemed to make many versions, elaborately rewriting each one for a week or so, and then either printing it out or starting over without printing it. Either way, Mr. X's memory of the plot would be wiped out when that version was wiped out of the word processor. Whatever was happening while he hallucinated tended to be wiped out of his memory too."

"That's a positively outrageous theory," said the Oldest Member, who could not even type, much less use a word processor. "It's obvious that Mr. X is a compulsive editor in a boring job who invented SF trash in his unconscious in order to have the dubious pleasure of editing it in his conscious and end up feeling like a superior editor conquering an inferior writer."

"Hmm," said the Interpersonal. "Perhaps that's a better theory than mine. It certainly speaks deeply to my unconscious."

"Very funny," said the Oldest Member. "You were probably going to speculate irrationally about the various metal objects in and on Mr. X's body forming with his nervous system an unusual electronic field capable of tuning into word processors being used someplace else."

"That's a perfectly possible theory," said one of the older

Pshrinks. "I'm not supposed to go near microwave ovens or garage doors that are activated by remote control devices. They futz up my own pacemaker."

"Nothing went wrong with Mr. X's pacemaker," said the Youngest Member.

"It was probably the last link that created the field," said the Interpersonal.

"There! You see! She's off and running with her own theory now that you've given her the chance," said the Oldest Member.

The Youngest hurriedly passed the largest helping of the newly arrived dessert, Freudian Fig Fling, to the Oldest Member.

The Interpersonal was muttering quietly to herself. "Endless revisions. Probably requested. Lines marching across the screen, disappearing and reforming. Oh, the agony."

"Well, I do think there's a point to this word processor theory," said the Youngest Member bravely, now that the Oldest was immersed in figs. "It must have been a very strange word processor, not in English, but in some unknown language like bird tracks and mysterious hieroglyphics, a language that when used in the machine could create the whole story—like a film—inside the head of anyone tied into the field."

The Oldest Member began turning purple and chewing rapidly.

"Colleagues," said the Interpersonal gravely. "Consider the possibilities. We humans are not alone in the universe. Somewhere out there are writers working on the equivalent of word processors."

"Hard-working writers," said a Pshrink who was trying to be one.

"Writers who have to revise and revise," said a Ph.D. Pshrink who had taken twenty years to write his thesis and felt superior to the M.D. Pshrinks who had never written any.

"Writers who drive editors berserk," said another who held tenaciously to his position as editor of one of the leading psychoanalytic journals.

The Youngest Member grinned at the Interpersonal and said, "I wish Mr. X hadn't had his fillings replaced. It sounds as if the story was turning out to be good after all."

The Oldest Member swallowed and said, "Listen here! There are *no* alien word-processors and there are *no* fantastic, alien writers."

"Oh?" said the Interpersonal. "I think I even know a few."

THE HOTTER FLASH

A strangely placid atmosphere prevailed at Pshrinks Anonymous. In the midtown hotel's subbasement dining room, there was such an unnatural calm that, for once, the official name of the weekly luncheon club—the Psychoanalytic Alliance—seemed apt.

Nobody's definition of deep analysis was in dispute. Insidiously possible entanglements with outer space were not even mentioned. Only a brief flurry of diatribes erupted against various editors who had rejected manuscripts produced by various Pshrinks fancying themselves to be gifted with literary talent. There was even a dearth of intriguing case material and not one good argument over theory.

Conversationally uncontroversial meetings like this one were, admittedly, rare. Not uncoincidentally, the Oldest Member was late.

One of the middle-aged Eclectics poked at his Chicken

Curry Climacteric and asked, "Where's the chutney? Why is the food so bland?"

"Today all interactions including gustatory ones have been, as we say in the trade, conflict-free," said a neo-Freudian whose forthcoming paper on the subject was supposed to be long and definitive, not that there was any other kind.

The door opened and the Oldest Member strode in, his white moustache waxed to fine points that tilted upward. He called for his lunch, surveyed his colleagues with his well-known Freudianly penetrating gaze, pulled a cigar from his breast pocket, and said as he twirled it under his nose:

"You all look bored, which means that superegos are rigid, ids are frustrated, and the no-smoking rule is still in force."

A chorus of cigar-addicted compatriots muttered assent.

"I think it's time to vote again on the rule," said the Oldest Member, raising his voice. Then he glanced sideways at the Pshrink sitting to his left. "How about that?" he said to her. "Are you going to fight for your rule?"

There was no answer.

"Hey! I realize you have a negative transferential reaction to me and my cigar but—"

"What?" said the Interpersonal, blinking at him as if she had not noticed his entrance, much less his call to battle. "I'm sorry. I was preoccupied in thinking about an unusual case."

The Oldest Member pursed his lips. "I want a vote on smoking. Will this case report take long?"

"Oh no. I will be forced to be discreetly brief, because this report is about an afflicted relative."

"Indeed. Brief, you say?" said the Oldest Member, sniffing his cigar voluptuously.

"I promise," said the Interpersonal. "I would not even mention the case except that I'm so upset about it and"—she smiled shyly at the Oldest Member—"you are always so helpful in promoting and analyzing the emotional catharsis of a fellow Pshrink."

Although he had winced when a female Pshrink called herself a "fellow," the Oldest Member nodded, expanded his chest, and then beamed happily at her. "You may be assured that this will remain indubitably confidential. We of P.A. are always eager to help with members' families, so often psychoanalytically neglected. I will be only too glad to interview your unfortunate relative—"

"Unfortunate is not exactly the operative word," said the Interpersonal, "although my Great-aunt Efferna died a few years ago. She was in her eighties at the time and went out smiling, after saying that she was pleased to be accomplishing genuine transcendence. The family was perturbed that she returned to her previous mystic tendencies on her deathbed, but on the whole they were relieved."

"I don't understand. Why is this a problem to you now?" said the Oldest Member, putting his cigar back into his breast pocket and popping a Shrimp Sigmund past his moustache.

"Perhaps I'd better tell the whole story," she said as the rest of the members groaned and called for the next course, Torte Nectarine a la Necromania.

My older relatives [said the Interpersonal] constituted a large assortment of diverse personages, none of whom ever flipped their lids in any certifiable way, but who represented a psychological challenge to any child who wanted to understand people. In fact, if a kid didn't figure out these relatives early in life, he or she was likely to become one of them, which is a possible explanation of how I got interested in becoming a Pshrink.

When I was growing up, this Efferna was my mother's sole remaining aunt, the spoiled youngest of many siblings in a family still psychodynamically attached to Victorian times. Efferna, their last bloom, was only ten years older than my own mother, but she obviously belonged to another epoch, which makes it even stranger that she didn't go backward instead of forward.

"Why have you stopped?" asked a Kleinian. "And what do you mean by that last sentence?"

"It's embarrassing," said the Interpersonal.

"Come now," said the Oldest Member. "Persevere."

First I must describe my great-aunt. In youth she was a tiny woman, well shaped but unable to demonstrate sex appeal because she seemed so maidenly high-strung, with enormous blue eyes staring in a bewildered way at a world that persisted in appalling her. No doubt her first marriage appalled her, because when widowhood came early, she seemed relieved.

The rest of the family had its turn to be appalled, because Efferna achieved widowhood in the depths of the Great Depression, when jobs were not available, especially not to a flighty lady with no work experience. Since her husband had died broke and there were no children to help, Efferna's many nieces and nephews passed her around.

She always stayed with us from Thanksgiving through New Year's, when her niece (my mother) would be trying to cope with the unluckily central location of our family, which attracted relatives from other geographical points to our house as a meeting place. Efferna, who talked and wrote with a profusion of capitals and italics, believed that she was a great asset during Major Holidays when the children were Home from School.

When I was young I thought Efferna was an asset, too, although some years later I realized that perhaps she was inclined to be a trial, as I overheard my mother remark. The problem was not that she thought she was a great cook—she was—or that she wrote poetry and read reams of it at each holiday to whatever herd of relatives and their friends she could corral in whatever living room she was currently in-habiting.

As my father was heard to say many times, the main problem was that Efferna was dangerously imaginative. This was rapidly compounded by what my mother and Efferna's other nieces (often in solemn conclave) referred to as "the change."

I was too young to know what this meant, but Efferna explained it to me in dubiously graphic detail when I incautiously asked her what she was changing into. Since I would listen, I was usually the recipient of her many vivid narrations; and according to my own analysis, it probably took me years to recover from the multiple misconceptions about life that Efferna implanted . . .

"We are not interested in your analysis," said an Adlerian grumpily. "Besides, it's against the club rules."

"Sorry about that," said the Interpersonal.

At any rate, Efferna went into menopause with a bang. Literally. She came back to our house one day announcing that a large Studebaker had *withered* her youth by backfiring just as she was passing behind it on her way from the public library, where she spent most of her time reading suspect fiction like the wilder products of H. G. Wells. The Studebaker's blast had been so loud that she had felt her insides shrivel and she said she would Never Be The Same Again.

My mother told my father that Efferna had been drying up—menstrually speaking—for some time, but the fact remained that Efferna never was the same again. Her periods stopped completely; and, like 80 percent of all human females, she began to suffer from hot flashes. Perhaps "suffer" is not the correct word. While "enjoy" might be too strong, it's on the right track.

"Hand me my fan, dear," she would say as she loosened

her neckline and flapped her arms like a triumphant hen. She could never remember the names of any of her grand-nieces, but that had nothing to do with premature senility (Efferna had every one of her unusual marbles). The entire family knew that Efferna had always been too preoccupied with what she called Higher Planes Of Thought to be able to concentrate on practical reality.

I would find her special fan, a large black object passed down from generation to generation that opened to a spar-kle of exotic flowers traced in gilt and outlined by thin strips of mother-of-pearl. Great-aunt Efferna told me that the fan was essential for ladies passing through "the change," and eventually wore it dangling on a black silk cord across her bosom in readiness for the next moment she was struck by a hot flash.

"I'm having another one," she would say possessively, fan-ning herself as she turned slightly pink and moist. "Let me tell you about the possibility of astral voyages during *un-usual* psychic states." She had begun a fervent study of sev-eral mystic books considered borderline even in the thir-ties . . .

"You're such a diehard rationalist," said one of the younger Interpersonals. "How did someone like that get in your family?"

"It would be more appropriate to ask how my family man-aged to get someone like me," said the Interpersonal.

. . . but no one paid any attention to her except me, and I was interested only because I'd been given a new Oz book for my seventh birthday and thought that astral voyages might be one way to get there. I soon learned, however, that Efferna thought of astral voyages as ways of getting out-of-the-body trips in the here and now, so one day between Christmas and New Year's during that hot flash winter, I decided to pin her down.

"Aunt Ef, where would you go on an astral voyage?"

She blotted her forehead with an embroidered handkerchief and fanned harder. The mother-of-pearl blended with the gilt and black to become a hypnotic pattern in the air.

"I haven't decided. I could go over and assassinate that Perfectly Awful man who is *ruining* Europe, but I don't speak German, and I really think I ought to give him a Piece Of My Mind first. Besides, I'm not at all Certain about what's feasible during such a voyage."

"What do you think could be possible?"

"Perhaps nothing but *observation*. I should not underestimate the Powers of Observation, of course; but Being Out of the Body may well be an *unnerving* experience, especially if one is helpless to change anything, being not present in physical form."

"But how can one travel anywhere without a body?" I would ask, for the umpteenth time.

"You are not old enough to understand," said Efferna, duplicating the refrain I heard from every relative older than I was.

New Year's Eve came, a particularly balmy night for December 31. At the inevitable large party taking over our house like a disease, Efferna startled everyone by refusing to read her poetry.

"I've torn most of it up. I'm starting over," she announced. Plucking a small bottle of champagne from a cooler, she waved vaguely to the other guests and ascended the staircase, over which several of us in the youngest generation were leaning to spy on the grown-ups. Our great-aunt swept past us and disappeared into the spare room, where she began to chant loudly.

"She's into Sanskrit again," said my father.

"Go to bed, children," said our mothers.

My bed was next to the wall of the spare room, so it was difficult to sleep with a lively and only slightly middle-aged great-aunt chanting on the other side. Soon, however, the sound of the grown-ups downstairs toasting the new year and singing "Auld Lang Syne" drowned out Efferna, and I went to sleep.

I woke up an hour later with the moonlight streaming across my face. The cousins staying over in my room were asleep, and I couldn't help thinking it was a grand night for an astral voyage. I tiptoed out of my room, peered over the stair at the grown-ups, all quietly playing bridge, and went to Efferna's room to find out if she'd made it.

Her room was empty. So was the bathroom. I looked through the upstairs but she and her fan were not there, although her clothes were hanging over a chair and her frilly negligee was at the foot of the bed. In the old mattress was an indentation as perfect as if Efferna were still there and had not dented down or rumpled the side of the bed in getting out.

Suddenly I was positive that she actually was still there but I couldn't see her. I decided that she'd achieved Out of the Body travel with the interesting complication of leaving her body behind in an invisible state. Quietly, I moved to the bed and stretched out my hand to touch her.

She wasn't there. The astral voyage theory hadn't scared me, but the sudden dissolution of it gave me a fright. I ran back to my room and woke up my oldest cousin.

"You idiot," she said predictably after hearing my story. "Having hot flashes is probably enough to push a silly old woman around the bend. She's probably been taken off to the booby hatch, which is okay by me because I won't have to listen to any more of that awful poetry or get embarrassed the way I was when she recited it to my boyfriend just as we were trying to leave for the seventh-grade dance . . ."

I went downstairs and got onto my father's lap.

"Have you sent Great-aunt Efferna to the booby hatch?"

"Good grief!" said my mother.

"Should I?" asked my father.

"I don't think so," I said, remembering that I had overheard my parents whispering about something called a psychiatric consultation. "But she's disappeared."

"Nonsense," said my mother. "She's in her room."

"She's not."

My father sighed. He was, I realize now, only in his early thirties, and he didn't like any kind of poetry except Rudyard Kipling. "You've both forgotten the back staircase."

So I had. It was usually blocked up with packages and cartons my mother hid in there at the last minute before guests arrived.

"And there's a full moon!" I said. My father winked at me, patted me on the behind, and sent me up to bed somehow convinced that my great-aunt would naturally want to escape outdoors to look directly at the full moon, especially on a warm New Year's Eve.

I went upstairs, wondered if perhaps Efferna might have had a voyage that was literally astral, or at least lunar. I peeked into her room, but there she was, sound asleep and clutching her black fan. I was disappointed.

I never caught her disappearing again, but later that year when she was staying with other relatives, she was taken to see a psychiatrist because she would unaccountably leave for short periods and return talking nonsense. Family discussion began about the inevitability of sending great-aunt for in-patient treatment, but quite suddenly she cleared up.

Her hot flashes stopped, practicality descended to quench her mysticism, and she found herself a husband, a rather gently dotty painter who achieved his own practicality during the war years by helping to build war planes while Efferna planted Victory gardens.

It was not until she was quite elderly that I learned about what happened to her during her brief months of menopausal vasomotor irregularity. At first she said she wanted to tell me because I'm a Pshrink and it might be useful someday in case it happened to anyone else, who'd then be in danger of being diagnosed crazy.

"I hope you're not going to try to persuade us that she actually went on astral voyages," said the Oldest Member.

"Aren't you?" asked a Jungian plaintively.

Great-aunt Efferna stated definitely that she had not gone on astral voyages during her hot flashes. "Balderdash," she said with a snort, having become much more bombastically assertive in old age. "Even Wells would not have approved of popping around the world totally Out of the Body, *interfering* in the lives of people on this planet that you know or might meet. It is not Proper."

"On this planet? You don't mean that you think you went to another planet?"

"What would I want to do that for? Space exploration may be important, and I'm glad I lived to see it now, but it's not as important as—but perhaps I'd better not tell you. I wouldn't want to Interfere with the Future any more than . . ."

"Do what? With what?"

"I suppose you break into your patients' sentences like that," she said with a sniff, even more ominous than the snort. "Now as I was saying before I was so Rudely Interrupted . . ."

I relaxed. She always said that when the moment of annoyance had passed.

". . . I was talking about the Future. Only now it's getting to be the present. My, I have enjoyed myself, though."

I stared at her. She certainly had looked happy during her postmenopausal years. Throughout the vicissitudes of personal aging in a troubled world, Efferna had remained sane, helpful, and so unremittingly cheerful that my parents often whispered about what a trial it was. She had also gone back to writing poetry, or rather gone on, for her postmenopausal verse was humorous, sold well, and gained her some notoriety.

"Aunt Ef, are you telling me that during your hot flashes you think you went bodily into the future?"

"With my fan. And only when I was strictly alone. It Would Not Do to disappear when anyone could see it happen. It's odd, however, that nowadays I don't seem to have so many *inhibitions* and I would enjoy seeing the reactions of other people, but of course it's too late. What a pity that I had such a *short* menopause."

"You think that you waved your fan . . ."

"Oh, vigorously, my dear, quite *vigorously*. It took practice. And one could never count on knowing exactly when a hot flash would come. That's why I had to start wearing the fan all the time so I wouldn't mislay it." She gazed complacently at her glass-doored cabinet, where the open fan had always reposed postmenopausally in dust-free spangled splendor.

"How could a fan—"

"Put anyone into the future?" Efferna smiled. "Perhaps it couldn't do it for just *anyone*. This is a *very* old fan, and it has presumably accumulated a great deal of Psychic Energy, which, when combined at a certain speed with the Aura given off by a *hotter* flash . . ."

"Now, Aunt Ef," I said reprovingly, as if I had somehow become the elder. Pshrinks tend to get that way, I've noticed, especially with friends and family. "I don't imagine that your hot flashes could have been hotter than anyone else's. My gynecological experience shows . . ."

"Pish!" said Aunt Efferna with another snort. "Doctors don't know anything. I lived through it, and I know that my hot flashes certainly were hotter. Perhaps"—she looked slyly at me—"it runs in our family."

"I wouldn't know," I said. "I'm not old enough, and my mother had very mild ones."

"Poor soul," said Efferna. "Perhaps it skips generations. I wouldn't have missed it for anything."

"The hot flashes?"

"The trips into the future."

"But what happened when you went into the future?" I cried, forgetting to insert the words "think you" between the "you" and the "went," as every good Pshrink must do in putting questions to people of doubtful sanity.

"At first I just observed. I glanced at newspapers, looked at television—that sort of thing."

"Back in the thirties you knew that television would be omnipresent now?"

"Yes. You'll have to admit that I made rather shrewd investments in the stock market at certain times."

It was well known in the family that Great-aunt Efferna had indeed become a financial wizard in her mature years, and was now rolling in it.

"You might have told the rest of us!"

"I tried to, but no one would listen to what I thought were *good* investments. Furthermore, I was terribly tempted to try to nip television In The Bud, but I couldn't think of what to do about it that wouldn't also change other things I didn't *want* changed."

I, of course, was terribly tempted to ask her what things she didn't want changed; but I didn't wish to seem to be taking the whole thing seriously. I had my professional reputation as a Pshrink to think of, even with dotty relatives. I thought of something else to ask that would catch her in fabrication.

"Didn't people notice you, Aunt Ef?"

"They didn't at first, although I was definitely there in the flesh and could perform *certain actions*. I was not an Out of the Body Projection, but somehow no one would see me very well. They would step aside but not really *notice* me. At first I was offended, but then I decided I was simply not in *tune* with the future universe because I was from their past."

"That must have been frustrating," I said sarcastically.

"Not for long. I figured out that since it was all a matter of the Proper Vibrations, I learned to tune in at certain times so that I could be seen and heard."

I remembered that Efferna had been heavily into mystic vibrations in her day. "What years did you go to, then? What did you see?"

"Oh, I wouldn't want to spoil it for you by going into details. Besides, it wasn't so much what I saw as what I eventually did."

"You mean you think that you made changes?"

"With, I suspect, far-reaching consequences. After all, it was an important international meeting, and although I was in my nightgown when I appeared, it was my *best* one, and they seemed attentive when I gave them a Piece of My Mind."

"But what did you say?"

She acted as if she had not heard me. Humming to herself, she opened the cabinet and took out the fan.

"Aunt Ef . . ."

Fanning herself gently, she looked at me as if scrutinizing the expression on my face. "Do you believe me?"

Much as I loved Great-aunt Efferna, I couldn't lie to her. "I don't know," I said.

"Good. Always keep an open mind and stick to truth. It may help in the forthcoming world upheaval—but I don't want to say any more. You, or someone you'd tell it to, might try to change what I've already changed and that would confuse things. You see, I am convinced that I have *improved* matters, although I won't live to see the changes I made in the future."

"You mean you're talking about what *hasn't* happened *yet?*" I said, lapsing into italics.

"That is correct, dear niece-once-removed."

"I think you mean grandniece."

"To be sure," she said, fanning a little harder. "You see, it would be Most Unpleasant to encounter one's past self, don't you think? I know that the future I visited is Yet To Come, and by then I will be *safely* dead."

"Safely?"

Suddenly she handed me her fan and said, "Take this, dear. You may find it—*useful.*"

"But Aunt Ef, I want to know what you *did!*"

"Try to enjoy life," said Great-aunt Efferna, and then she began to laugh.

The Oldest Member pushed aside his coffee cup, grabbed one end of his moustache for support, and said, "That's one of the most incomplete case histories I have ever heard!"

The Interpersonal seemed to be staring off into an unknown distance.

"Were you able to estimate what year your great-aunt might have appeared?" asked a rather unsuccessful Pshrink, who always thought that his patients were telling the truth.

The Interpersonal shook her head.

The Oldest Member peered closer at her, his frown metamorphosing into a look of professional concern. "What's the matter? Are you upset? It's not your fault that your great-aunt was so clearly neurotic."

"I know, but there are complications," said the Interpersonal.

"Let me help," said the Oldest Member, still exercising his consultative powers and taking a deep breath as if he meant to go on for some time. "However sad it was that your family neglected to obtain prolonged treatment for your disturbed relative—with a reliable Pshrink—I can assure you that the whole case was probably just a simple problem of reorganizing the libido . . ."

"Have you noticed," interrupted one of his colleagues, also addicted to cigars, "that lunch is over and we've never gotten around to voting on the no-smoking rule?"

The Oldest Member expelled his breath forcefully, causing his moustache to flare out like an angry porcupine. "Now see here! I think—"

"Wait," said the Interpersonal. "There really is a genuine ongoing problem." Rummaging in her purse, she extracted a long black fan. When she opened it, the mother-of-pearl and painted gilt flowers glistened.

"A problem?" said the Oldest Member, raising his eyebrows.

"But don't worry, I've resigned myself to solving it now that I've started getting hot flashes," said the Interpersonal cheerfully as she fanned herself—with vigor.

A MILLION SHADES
OF GREEN

After a frigidly protracted winter, a procrastinative spring generates in many Manhattanites the strange need to consult psychoanalysts—who are then assumed to be happily making money hand over id because everyone else is unhappy. Nevertheless, the Psychoanalytic Alliance luncheon club was far gone in gloom.

Even a casual glance at the faces of those members of Pshrinks Anonymous who were morosely toying with their Veal Chops Venera sufficed to prove that making money isn't everything and that, like normal New Yorkers, Pshrinks get depressed by a long winter too.

"Hell's bells," said the Oldest Member. "I hate snow in April."

"It's only April 1," said one of his more obsessively logical Freudian colleagues, "and snow on April Fool's Day is not uncommon."

"Then it behooves us not to be fools," said an Eclectic with a notably recent tan. "One must accept things as they are."

"Oh? Then why did you spend the last three weeks in the Caribbean?" said the Oldest Member grumpily, spearing an overcooked Asparagus Anaclitic.

"Why not? Any successful Pshrink could do the same," said the Eclectic, ordering another Bourbon Bleuler.

As the Oldest Member scowled and cleared his throat with an ominously bass rumble, one of the female Pshrinks tapped him lightly on his impeccably tweeded forearm.

"Did I ever tell you," said the Interpersonal, "about the conversations on early spring that I had with a Martian?"

"Pay no attention to her," said the Oldest Member.

She reached down to touch a large, flat, rectangular package wrapped in brown paper, leaning against her chair. "Since we are all eager to see spring, perhaps it would be of interest if I explained how important all the various shades of green can be . . ."

"I think I'll smoke," said the Oldest Member, grabbing his cigar from his breast pocket.

This time the Interpersonal did not need to admonish him, for the job was done by the other nonsmokers, whose militancy rose with every new medical article on the subject.

"Very well, I abide by the rule," said the Oldest Member, "but I'm leaving. Lunch is appalling, the company is depressing, and my wife made me wear my galoshes today."

"I want to hear about the conversations with a Martian," said one of the younger Pshrinks.

"Is it a story full of boring adjectival descriptions about spring?" said another P.A., who was known to be writing a novel.

"Verbosity is an epidemic disease in spring but I'll try to

control myself," said the Interpersonal, turning to the Oldest Member, who had risen. "Please stay. This is a true story, more or less, and I think you've heard about this particular Martian."

The Oldest Member groaned and sat down.

No matter which month spring picks for actual arrival [said the Interpersonal], there are always early signs that the season is about to explode: the willows around the boating pond vibrate with color; shoots pop up from underground bulbs; any city tree that has survived the winter begins to look hazy as its buds swell and crack open; male pigeons— like most males—puff up and strut.

Many years ago, at just this time of year, I first met a patient I will call Mr. M. He was a little dumpling of a man, with the face of a slightly demented kewpie doll . . .

"What's a kewpie doll?" asked the Youngest Member, the token psychiatric resident.

. . . and those too young to remember kewpie dolls should be sad that they missed those appealing little creatures. Mr. M had the same air of innocent knowingness in his cherubic face, as if he could be pleasant to have around no matter what mischief he might think up.

I was on my first job out of residency, running a locked psychiatric ward at one of the local hospitals. Mr. M had been in many psychiatric wards since his premature discharge from the Army, but he had only recently moved to New York. To the surprise of the admitting office personnel, when they told Mr. M that he was being assigned to the ward of a certain doctor I shall call Blank, this newcomer of a patient promptly fell prone on the floor and sobbed.

Since Mr. M was supposed to be actively hallucinating and potentially suicidal, the young doctor on admissions duty that night decided not to strain things any more than they were. He assigned Mr. M to the other locked ward—mine.

When I arrived next morning to see what flotsam had been cast up on the shores of our little hospital universe during the night shift, I found Mr. M operating with whimsical reasonableness; organizing a patients' work committee, starting a ward newspaper, acting as if there were no earthly reason why he had ever been admitted. The aides were already muttering about how overcrowded the ward was, especially with patients healthy enough to be on one of the open wards.

"According to the admitting office diagnosis," said the head nurse, "he's hallucinating, but he won't say what."

At that point Dr. Blank entered my office, looking over his shoulder as was his wont. He was a tall, thin, nervous ectomorph who for years had been running the other locked ward with discipline honed to a fine art. Residents assigned to do therapy on his ward complained that Dr. Blank never saw the patients personally unless in the presence of strong male aides and nurses equipped with instant injectables.

Dr. Blank was, of course, not a Pshrink. He was merely an adequate administrative psychiatrist who never intended to open a private practice.

"I see by the daily admitting roster that you've got Mr. ———," said Dr. Blank. "Watch out for him. I had him as a patient in an army hospital. Once when he was working in the kitchen he scraped all the mold off the old bread, made a ball of it, and threw it at me. And you know how allergic I am!"

Dr. Blank's allergies were legendary. He permitted no plants to adorn his ward, and was constantly inspecting for possible molds. The staff tended to say that Dr. Blank was allergic to anything alive.

I dragged out Mr. M's skimpy admitting chart. "What's the matter with this patient?" I asked timidly. Dr. Blank was also notorious for disapproving of female psychiatrists, and of Pshrinks. I was already the first and rapidly becoming the second.

Dr. Blank sneezed, glared at the plants on my windowsill, and said, "That patient thinks he's a Martian." After this stunning announcement, Blank hurried out.

Now during my recent psychiatric residency training, I had finally discovered science fiction—late, I admit, but since I read fast I soon caught up and had covered the field. Martians were a bit old hat, but I hadn't met one yet.

"Send in Mr. M," I said to the head nurse.

"By himself? The admitting note says he might be dangerous."

"I think I'd rather talk to a Martian alone."

Mr. M bounced in. He was intelligent, literate, amusing, charming, and reluctant to talk about the Martian, who seemed to inhabit a portion of Mr. M's body roughly in the area where the spleen normally hangs out. Furthermore, Mr. M said I was not allowed to talk directly to the Martian.

He cocked his head on one side and said, "I hear you're not a bad Pshrink. Tell you what—I'll relay messages to the Martian if you behave yourself and don't get too nosy."

"Nosiness is part of my trade," I said.

"Does it upset you?" said Mr. M solicitously. "If you want to talk about it I'll be glad to listen. I've got until the ward meeting when I want to get a vote on new curtains for the day room . . ."

"I want to talk about the Martian," I said.

"You would. It's not polite."

"That has nothing to do with—"

"Now now, temper, temper. Try to understand that the Martian doesn't approve of me going to hospitals."

"What does he approve of?"

Mr. M shrugged, his face blank.

I waited.

"The Martian," said Mr. M suddenly, in a whisper, "doesn't approve of me much at all."

"Why not?"

"I'm inadequate."

There was another silence. I could hear the head nurse and the ward secretary moving just outside my door, staying within shouting range in case I needed help. They were both bigger and stronger than I was, and since my arrival on the job they'd been trying to fatten me up.

I knew the patients' meeting would start all too soon. "Okay," I said, "but how can anyone be inadequate for a Martian?"

"He says I don't understand the full importance of capturing all the things that can be lost. I've tried—gee but I've tried. Everyone says I'm efficient at almost everything. Everyone but the Martian."

"What things that can be lost?"

"Like spring. Like the life on a planet. Mars is dead, all rocky and deserty, but it wasn't once."

Remember that this was long ago, before Voyager sent back pictures and took samples. In those days many respectable scientists still hoped that Mars possessed some plant life, if not higher creatures hiding in underground cities or wooded valleys.

"I always go crazy when spring starts," continued Mr. M. "The Martian plagues the devil out of me, and no matter how hard I try, I can't oblige. Sometimes I do crazier and crazier things, and I scare myself. I feel so sad . . ."

"Let me speak to this Martian," I said firmly, for Mr. M's protruding lower lip was beginning to tremble, and I didn't want Dr. Blank to find out that I'd failed to keep Mr. M from sobbing his heart out on my floor.

"He doesn't want to talk to you. He says to ask you what you want to find out."

"I want to find out why the Martian picked on you."

There was silence while Mr. M shut his eyes and his lips stopped quivering and started to move silently.

"He says it's because I could be a great artist."

"How does he know that?"

There was a longer silence. I will not, from now on, report the entire three-way process of communicating with the Martian, but you should remember that it proceeded in this manner.

"He says he's not actually sure, but it seems I have an unusual ability to perceive variations in colors."

"Is that true?" I asked.

Mr. M smiled. "Perhaps. The few paintings I've sold were to people who admired the colors. Actually this is a terrible problem to me. I can never make a painting exactly the way it should be—oh, I'm not fussy about line and arrangement and all sorts of things like that, for I think I do them well enough and it's an individual matter, but it kills me not to get colors right. I resent the Martian's insistence that I can do it even better. The colors, I mean."

"Do you act crazy to prove to him that you can't paint better?"

"That's crap."

"Only you know that."

"I'm fifty-nine and I don't know anything. I suppose you think you know everything. How old are you?"

"Twenty-nine," I said. "Right now I don't know much because you won't tell me much. I don't know anything about Martians and even less about painting."

"Maybe you'll learn," said Mr. M, suddenly the cheerful, gray-haired child who had been bustling about the ward. "But the Martian says to tell you not to try to be so smart-ass. We bet that you can't get along with Dr. Blank any better than we can."

"Well . . ."

"Don't worry about it. Dr. Blank can't help being a prick. He's scared of me, you know, because I'm freer than he is, even if I am possessed by a Martian every spring."

"Aha!" I said, intending to change the subject as soon as possible because I didn't like Dr. Blank very much either, and might easily have been tempted to lie down on the floor and cry if I'd had to work on his ward. "So you're only possessed in spring?"

"Well, isn't that obvious? Oh—I guess you haven't gotten my old charts yet."

"No."

"You'll see. Only in spring." He paused, rolled his eyes upward for a full minute, and then smiled at me. "You don't get scared when I hallucinate."

"I thought you said you were inhabited by a Martian."

"But any Pshrink would say I hallucinate."

"True. What does the Martian say about that?"

"He's not interested, although it amuses him that you're the first psychiatrist who's wanted to talk to him."

"May I?"

"Just now he told me that he thought perhaps you could be trusted—eventually."

"Then can we get back to the subject of spring?"

Mr. M blinked. "I have to go to the ward meeting."

"Please, about spring . . ."

"Have you actually sent for my old charts?"

"Of course."

"It'll take a while for them to come from all those other hospitals. In the meantime," he rubbed his hands gleefully, "I have so much to do here."

"But about spring . . ."

Mr. M blew me a kiss and bobbed out of my office.

The charts did take a long time in arriving. I interviewed Mr. M once more before they arrived, but although he gave me a précis of his childhood, adolescence, and college years, he shut up on the subject of the Army, and refused to reveal what happened in spring.

"No, Doc. It's the Martian's problem, and I don't have his permission to talk about it, although I've given you a hint. Just remember that I've never hurt anyone or myself."

"Why are you telling me that?"

"Because the Martian wants me to work hard for an in-hospital pass so I can go to the Occupational Therapy section to improve my painting. In fact, he says you should give every nonviolent patient a pass if the big brass won't let you make this an open ward."

So he'd found out what I'd been trying to do since I took the job. I knew that my chances of turning the ward into an unlocked one were nil, but I had succeeded in instituting in-hospital passes. I had even begun to think of them as little bits of largess I could hand out as if from on high, feeling very important because Dr. Blank did not permit passes of any kind from his ward.

"Will Your Majesty consider giving me a pass?" said Mr. M.

Shamefaced, I said, "I'll think about it."

He laughed, a lock of fine gray hair falling down over one eye. He winked at me with the other, got up, and told me to study his records carefully when they arrived because he had explained his history enough already.

"Can't you at least tell me about spring?"

"I have to create pictures," said Mr. M in cheerful resistance. Then he pattered back to the ward to commandeer for himself all the available colored chalks, the only kind of art equipment allowed on a locked ward.

By the day his records arrived, Mr. M had produced several exceptional pictures in chalk, on upside-down pages of the New York *Times* classified section, which provided a gently weird background for his work. I decided that he was not exactly a totally abstract expressionist because one could detect tongue-in-cheek renditions of various human frailties that made you smile when you saw the pictures.

I studied the records carefully. Mr. M had been a success-ful commercial artist before World War II, when he was shipped to North Africa during that campaign in the desert. He was wounded slightly and although he apparently healed quickly, he became unable to draw maps and other things assigned to him in his special duty. Gradually it was appar-

ent that he was talking feverishly to himself and he was sent
to a hospital for observation.

There it was noted that he could write or draw with his
dominant hand—the right—but could color only with his
left. Nowadays we would say that his right and left cortical
areas (the intuitive and logical sides of the brain, corre-
sponding to left and right hands in right-handed people) had
become psychologically separated in his art.

He became obsessed with certain paints and one day ate
them all, necessitating gastric lavage. He told the doctors
that a Martian made him do it. To use an unfortunately
popular medical expression, everything progressed rapidly
downhill after that, and he stayed hospitalized for some
time.

Mr. M then spent many years in V.A. psychiatric clinics,
receiving psychotherapy which seemed to work in spite of
Mr. M's reluctance to divulge anything of significance about
his problems. Mr. M was able to earn a living as a mail-sorter
in the post office, he volunteered his services as an art
teacher to disabled veterans, and had a blameless life—except that once a year he would have a brief psychotic episode requiring another brief hospitalization.

In spite of the voluminous records on Mr. M, I felt that I
still didn't know what had really happened to him. I consulted Dr. Blank.

"I don't want to talk about that guy. It's all in the records."

"It isn't."

"It was a long time ago and I can't remember much."

"Weren't you in North Africa during the war, too?" I
asked.

"Great place. My allergies disappeared—until I was reas-
signed to that hospital where Mr. M threw the mold at me,
saying I could try blue-green algae if I couldn't be enthusias-
tic about green life."

"Green?" I asked, mostly to keep the conversation going
in an approved Pshrink manner.

"Um, yes. I wanted to give him shock treatment, but he was committed to a Veterans' hospital here in the Northeast, one that was out in the country surrounded by repulsive vegetation full of pollen and molds. Apparently he thrived there, for he was eventually discharged as cured—but of course we know better."

I was still persevering on green. "I don't suppose that it was green paint that Mr. M ate?"

"All the green paints."

"But why?"

"He has an idiotic obsession with the color green," said Dr. Blank with a sneer. "He claims veteran's benefits on the grounds that the desert warfare turned him into a nut. He should be put away."

"You mean you don't think he's malingering?" (It was one of Dr. Blank's favorite diagnoses.)

"I thought he was at first, but you should have seen him on my ward after he threw the mold at me. He was soon talking only to his Martian, and the colors in his pictures got duller and duller until one day he painted on his bedsheets—can you imagine what with?"

"Yes," I said, feeling confident that under my competently enlightened management, Mr. M would do no such thing on *my* ward.

Dr. Blank rubbed his long bony fingers as if he were trying to join Lady Macbeth's cleanup campaign. "You'll be well advised to keep Mr. M locked up and, better yet, recommitted upstate. I think he's dangerous."

"But what about the Martian?"

"I trust that you mean Mr. M's hallucination. He would never tell me, or anyone else, much about it, but I once overheard him muttering that he was under assignment. It was so ridiculous that I never wrote it in the chart."

"Are you saying that he imagined a Martian had hired him to do something?"

"Yes. I think the job was to paint the kinds of green that

appear in early spring." Dr. Blank sneezed. "Allergens, all of them. The man's psychotic."

"But not everyone likes the desert."

"I loved it."

"Why are you here in the Northeast, then?" I said with my usual uncontrollable curiosity.

He squirmed in his chair. "My mother lives in a town house here in the city—and needs me. We have dinner together every night, she's thrown out the potted palms that she used to have, and . . . look here! You're not paying attention to the problem of your crazy patient! Keep him locked up. You're young and inexperienced and have never been in a desert—have you?"

"No."

"It takes a real man to live in the desert," said Dr. Blank, turning to the papers on his desk with a gesture of dismissal.

I went back to my ward and sent for Mr. M.

"Why did you avoid telling me about your real problem with spring? It wasn't in the records, but you must have known that Dr. Blank would tell me about your preoccupation with shades of green."

"Ah. My strange obsession. I've been in so many of these hospitals that I know the jargon. The Martian thinks the language is silly, but I rather enjoy it."

"Answer my question, please."

"Well, well, you're learning to be an authority figure!"

"And you are not exactly bucking for a work pass."

"I apologize, boss. The fact is that Dr. Blank is the real alien. As his allergist has undoubtedly told him, he was probably designed for a nongreen planet—perhaps Mars as it is now. Perhaps he lives with his mother—yes, I know a lot about everybody—because no one else wants to put up with him. There aren't any plants on his ward and he's always washing himself and spraying his nostrils and he doesn't understand the Martian and me."

"He doesn't know that," I said.

Mr. M nodded and leaned forward conspiratorially. "The Martian and me—and possibly you—are part of the web of life that is planet Earth, and once was Mars."

"Are you sure it's Mars?" I asked, responding to the faint tingling at the base of my spine that indicated I was being prodded by my psychoanalytic intuition—or possibly my overindulgence in science fiction.

There was a long silence while Mr. M massaged his silky gray hair with faintly green-tinted fingers. Then he heaved a sigh. "No, I'm not at all sure that it's Mars. I call him a Martian because he's been there, back when Mars was green, but I don't know—and I'm not going to ask—where he originated."

"But . . ."

"It doesn't matter, you know. He's an intelligent person who worries about keeping a planet green. He hates deserts. He wants me to paint the spring greens so that humanity will never forget how beautiful they are and never want to lose them."

I nodded, since Mr. M's hallucination agreed with my sentiments. "A few minutes ago you said 'the web of life that *is* planet Earth.' Did you mean it that way or did you mean to say 'on' Earth?"

"You're no kindred soul if you don't know that the web of life is Earth itself, coming alive, just as we are all parts of the universe coming alive."

"Yes," I said.

"May I have more shades of green chalk?"

"You may have a pass to the occupational therapy section, and I'll see that they provide plenty of green paints."

"If you're going to invent a story," complained a Pshrink, "couldn't you at least behave more analytically in it?"

"Go ahead and believe that it's just a story," said the Interpersonal, shoving her Orange Pudding Oedipus over to the Oldest Member, who was partial to it.

All went well for a few days [continued the Interpersonal]. Mr. M bobbed in and out of the ward on his pass, busy reorganizing occupational therapy and making intricate plans for a magnificent art show starring work done by patients, as well as that of whatever hospital personnel he deemed had any talent whatsoever.

It was obvious that Mr. M was very popular in the hospital —except with Dr. Blank—and everyone exclaimed over his cheerful efficiency, his wit, and his ability to rouse enthusiasm in depressed patients. I began to imagine that Mr. M's salvation would be in getting some training that might sneak him into a permanent hospital position.

His request for an outside pass was casual. He just wanted to go out of the hospital for a few hours and would be right back, for he had a lot to do in occupational therapy. Since he was on a locked ward still, it took a conclave of staff psychiatrists to pass on his pass. Only Dr. Blank voted against it, claiming that just because Mr. M no longer talked about his hallucinations didn't mean he wasn't having them. Since all of us knew plenty of people on the outside who hallucinated in a respectably quiet way, we disagreed with Blank.

The next day I was very busy with new admissions and hardly noticed when Mr. M took his pass and left the hospital for the few hours he had promised. I did not anticipate trouble, and I trusted that he would indeed return.

Which he did. I was working on charts and didn't see him.

The next thing I knew, my head nurse charged into my office as if propelled from a cannon. "You'd better come and look at our resident artist. He's back and he doesn't look good."

I found Mr. M sitting in his bathrobe in a dim corner of the day room, surrounded by crumpled sheets of the New York *Times* classified section, all covered with red chalk.

"Red?" I asked.

"Angry," he said, kicking at the papers with his childlike feet.

I took him to my office and said, "Couldn't you just tell me about it?"

"You're not an artist. You wouldn't understand."

"I'm part of the web of life, dammit. Tell me."

Mr. M wiped his eyes on his sleeve and shuddered. "It's no use. I can't do it. And I refuse to go back to those clinics for more therapy, week after week, year after year. I know what I'm like. It's no use."

I said nothing.

He blinked and scowled at me. "I went to Central Park for the whole day. Had hot dogs at the boat house. Saw migrating warblers all over the place. Spring is starting again, every tree bud beginning to open, every forsythia bush into yellow—that's all right, I can do yellow—but the damn greens are coming back and I swear the shades are more subtle and difficult than ever and I'm going to kill myself so the Martian will stop jeering at me because I'm a failure and I can't do it, I can't capture the million shades of green and I want to die . . ."

"Whoa! Now we'll work on this problem and in the meantime you'll stay here where there isn't any changing green."

"I can see the trees in the hospital's front yard and . . ."

"We will talk about them every day as they come into leaf, and please go on painting."

"You can't be my therapist. You're the ward psychiatrist and you aren't supposed to do anything but administrative work, and the new psychiatric residents won't be here until July first, and the only ones in the hospital right now are over on Blank's ward . . ."

"I admit we are short-staffed, but I will do my best."

"All right. I won't kill myself. It would upset the ward nurse anyhow, and I like him."

So Mr. M stayed on my ward, working in chalks on the New York *Times.* He had more colors than before because the occupational therapist thought he was adorable and bought some for him herself. He struggled on, and each day I tried to talk to him, while the Martian inside grew angrier and angrier, and Mr. M became more and more depressed.

Finally one day when the sun was warmer than usual and the trees were leafing out and it was clear that the early days of spring were moving on, I arrived at the hospital to find that Mr. M's painting for the evening before had been all in one particularly drab color. It was a stunningly violent abstraction, probably a masterpiece, but it smelled so we had to throw it out.

One of the more fastidious Kleinians put down his napkin and rose, saying, "I see no reason to listen to this sort of thing over lunch."

"Don't split," said the Oldest Member. "Think of it as only a projection."

"Didn't I tell you so?" said Dr. Blank in the staff lunchroom. "Now do you believe that he's committable?" One of his more prolonged sneezes exploded. "God, how I hate spring."

The next time I saw Mr. M for an interview the aides had to carry him into my office because he wouldn't walk. His head lolled on his shoulders, his eyes were vacant, and if spoken to, he cried.

"I don't want to talk to you," I said in desperation, wishing I were working at a place like Chestnut Lodge, where patients as sick as this could have intensive psychotherapy. "I want to talk to the Martian."

Mr. M snuffled.

Half an hour later, after I was hoarse from trying to be persuasive, Mr. M closed his eyes, looked as if he were asleep, but began to speak in another voice, deep and rich— so different that the hairs at the back of my neck seemed to lift.

"You want to know a lot," said the voice. "I permit you to ask a few questions."

I swallowed and hoped my voice wouldn't croak. "Were the greens on Mars—or wherever you come from—as beautiful as those of spring here on Earth?"

"More."

"Then perhaps nothing here will ever satisfy you," I said, with pity.

"I hadn't thought of that before. Why hadn't I?"

"I don't know. Perhaps you're homesick."

"My friend was homesick for green when he was trapped in the desert, wounded."

"Yes," I said, trying not to breathe more rapidly.

"He's a good artist."

"Not good enough for you?"

"No. It makes me angry. I have to punish him—and everyone."

"We're only Terrans. We can't help it."

"You take your living planet for granted."

"Not all of us. Perhaps none of us, really," I said.

"Why can't you cure my friend and make him the perfect artist who can transmit to a picture all the million shades of green?"

"You tell me."

"You mean you can cure him but won't tell me why you're not doing it?" said the voice furiously.

"You know damn well I don't cure anyone. People who get well may do it with a lot of help, but they do it themselves."

"But he can't cure himself!"

"Yes he can. He does it every year, except in spring."

"Then I make him go crazy."

"So it seems."

"Go to hell."

Mr. M suddenly seemed to wake up. He smiled at me and

said in his usual lilting tenor, "You're getting to him, Doc. Give *him* hell."

I smiled back. "But you like the Martian. Nobody else has understood how you suffered during the North African campaign."

"That's for sure. You know—I think the problem is that both he and I go crazy every spring, out of love for all the greens, out of wanting to possess them permanently—and they never last—hell, they never last, Doc! All at once they're gone and it's the deep uniform green of summer."

"Did you think, when you were in North Africa, that you'd never see the greens of our spring again?"

"Yes. A tank blew up near me and a piece of metal went into my eye. They took it out okay and my vision wasn't permanently damaged, but it could have been—I didn't mind the piece in my thigh or the scars from the burns I got, but to lose my eyesight—to think about losing it—did you know that the Martian can't see at all unless I look at things for him? That's why we have to go to the park every spring and study the shades of green and why he wants me to paint all of them . . ."

"Let me speak to him again," I said.

"Okay, but tell him I'm only human and I'm doing the best I can—just like you, Doc."

Mr. M's eyes stared into infinity while I talked to his Martian, who for the first few minutes used only obscenities, the sort that men who are men learn in a desert army, as an obbligato to my conversation.

". . . so you see, sir, you're not being fair," I concluded.

"What the hell kind of psychiatrist are you, anyway? What's fair—about what happened to Mars, or about what's happening to Earth—desertification, destruction, stupidity . . ."

"I think you want perfection," I said angrily. "A perfect artist. Maybe you should visit some other planet."

"I like this one."

"You need treatment—you know that."

"Humans need treatment!" he shouted.

"So what else is new?" I shouted back.

There was a long pause while Mr. M twitched the way animals do in their sleep when they are dreaming.

"What are you suggesting?" asked the Martian's voice, rather politely.

"Leave Mr. M alone for the rest of the year."

"I already do."

"You don't," I said earnestly, forgetting that quite probably there was no Martian. "You make him work at a job he's not suited for while you insist he must paint better than any human has ever been able to. Let him spend the year doing what he's good at and then . . ."

"Then what?" jeered the Martian.

"Then in early spring tell him to go to a therapist and the three of you hash out the problem. There's a lot of green left on Earth, you know. You don't have to make us all miserable just because the universe is short on green in other places."

"The greens are vanishing from Earth!"

"We'll try to save them. You'll try. But asking for perfection makes the task impossible. Have you found perfection anywhere in the universe?"

He was silent. The corners of Mr. M's mouth bent upward.

"How about it?" I asked. "Truce?"

"I'll think it over."

"You'd better." I closed the chart with a bang and felt more exhausted and incompetent than usual. Nevertheless, I knew intuitively that assigning Mr. M to more long-term therapy would be useless, although he was indubitably psychotic.

"Or the Martian was," said the Oldest Member.

"Why, I didn't know that you liked SF," said the Interpersonal.

"Harrumph!" said the Oldest Member.

Mr. M shook his head and rubbed his eyes. "I heard what you said to my Martian, Doc. He's stubborn and sort of stupid—a lot more stupid than I realized. But you tried hard."

"Thanks a lot," I said sourly.

"Maybe he can't help it. He's the last of his kind. Or perhaps the first—I don't know. I feel sorry for him. He's worse off than I was in North Africa."

Suddenly I felt inspired. "Why don't you take over his therapy, until each spring, of course."

Mr. M pursed his lips. "I think you're making a bargain with me. No one else did that before. I stay sane—until spring—and then I bring him in for therapy?"

"We could try it."

"I suppose it *is* up to me to cope with this alien, because he does like it here on Earth—I didn't know that before—and he's quite happy most of the year until spring comes—and goes, too quickly. What will you and I do every spring— review the progress I'm making on the Martian?"

"That's a good idea."

"Can I come to your private office? I'm sick of being a disabled vet."

"Okay."

"But I'm still worried about the million shades of green!" he said plaintively. A fat tear rolled down his cheek and his mouth crumpled.

"Teach the Martian how to enjoy them—in the brief moment of their existence. Being angry because they don't last will destroy that moment."

He wiped away the tear. "I suppose you could be right."

"Thanks."

"But wrong, too, because—hey! yes!—the memory of the colors lasts forever!"

"Even if minds don't."

"That's your opinion. The Martian and I know better. Memories stay in the web of life somehow. Look at Mars!"

The Interpersonal stopped speaking and reached for the plate of cookies that went with the pudding she had rejected.

The Oldest Member smiled and even chuckled softly, but surprised everyone by saying nothing.

"That's the end of the story?" asked the psychiatric resident. "Aren't you going to tell us what happened after that?"

"Mr. M was discharged a week or so after the conversation I have just reported," said the Interpersonal.

"But he must have been still hallucinating," said one of the more orthodox Pshrinks.

"Not exactly. He never hallucinated actively again except for a week in early spring. Then, as he had promised, he came to see me in my private practice. He never had to be hospitalized again, mainly—I think—because he felt sorry for the Martian. He went back to commercial art for a living, very successfully, for the wild coloration his left hand painted became nicely integrated with the drawing precision of his right hand. He also had a few moderately successful shows of his kooky paintings, the sort that are both charming and humorous. He was a happy man."

"Did you ever get a painting?"

"I told him he shouldn't give me one and I shouldn't buy one because I didn't want anything to interfere with the work we did. That was my intellectual reason. Actually I was afraid to know what I would choose or what he would give me. It doesn't matter now, since he died last fall at a respectably advanced age, peacefully, in his sleep. He left me this in his will, and oddly enough, I received it today."

She unwrapped the rectangular object that had been beside her chair and stood up holding the canvas so the Pshrinks Anonymous could see it.

With a gust that blew out his silver moustache, the Oldest Member expelled his breath in what may have been relief. "He must have known that no one could have done it better."

The Interpersonal nodded. "Early spring—all the greens —on canvas. I shall hang it in the entrance hall of my analytic institute so everyone can look at it and feel better."

The Oldest Member remained seated as the other Pshrinks left to return to their offices and the listening posts behind their couches.

The Interpersonal wrapped up the painting and said, "Care to tell the rest of the story?"

The Oldest Member grunted.

The Interpersonal adjusted her eyeglasses and peered at him. "I was given to understand that Dr. Blank eventually went into analysis."

"Um."

"He'd have been a tough case for anyone."

"Um. His analyst failed."

"I disagree," said the Interpersonal. "I heard that Dr. Blank ended up as a brilliant general-hospital administrator, having left psychiatry—clearly the wrong field for him."

"Um."

"It seems that he chose a therapeutic location for his new job. Wasn't it somewhere in the Southwest—in a desert area?"

"Some allergies are better in the desert," said the Oldest Member. "Some humans are more alien than others, I suppose."

"I've often thought that if there were aliens from outer space lurking around, it's probably because they're in love with our living planet. Of course, that cuts down on the drama, doesn't it?"

"Not at all. Come along," said the Oldest Member, rising.

"Let's walk through the park while I smoke my cigar, and take a look at the million shades of green coming up through the snow."

AUGUST ANGST

Pshrinks Anonymous had shrunk. There were so few people sitting around the lunch table at the weekly Psychoanalytic Alliance meeting that it was obviously the beginning of August.

"I don't know about the rest of you masochists," said the Oldest Member, spooning up Madrilene Mania, which—the air-conditioning being what it was—had lost its jell, "but *my* wife insisted on a July vacation for a change. I told her it was blasphemous, but here I am, working during the Angst of August."

"It doesn't seem so bad this year," said one of his Freudian colleagues. "In fact, most of my patients have taken August vacations and none of them have called me. No one is anxious enough to miss me, and I might as well have taken off two months the way my husband wanted."

"I feel the same way," said a member newly graduated from analytic school. "I decided to spend August baby-sitting the anxious patients of vacationing Pshrinks so I could make money to help pay off the expenses of analytic training, but I'm not at all busy."

"Naturally, at *my* fee rate," said the Oldest Member complacently, "I only have to see the more desperate patients, but there haven't been any so far, a far cry from my younger days when August Angst kept me solvent while I was building up my private practice."

One of the female Interpersonals, who had been toying with a noticeably limp stalk of celery, glanced at the erect waxed tips of the Oldest Member's moustache and said, "You seem impervious to heat in August."

"And you seem preoccupied," said the Oldest Member. "Hot flashes, or difficult patients?"

"Neither. I'm on vacation. What I was thinking about was whether or not there's anything to a certain famous SF story about the summer silly season, when mysterious events are not taken seriously."

"Balderdash," said the Oldest Member. "The only mystery is why my guests have not shown up, a young couple who are both analysts and moved to Manhattan recently to start practice. To tide them over they have jobs at Bellevue, where my niece met them and told them about me. I told her to send them here for lunch. I can't remember their name, so I can't call them to find out what's wrong."

The door to the subbasement dining room opened abruptly and a young woman entered. She was dressed in what ought to have been a decorously tailored, indeed a typically professional summer suit, but the unaided perfection of her figure announced itself through the sheer fabric of her blouse. Her hair was long and shining. Her complexion was clear and radiant. Her features might have tipped the scales in a Miss America contest.

All the male Pshrinks sat up straight. Even the celery looked less limp.

"Hi! Sorry I'm late. I'm Leora Hiddens. Just call me Leora."

There was a shocked silence, which the Interpersonal broke by saying gently, "At these meetings we try not to call or refer to each other—or anyone else—by name. It's sort of a club rule."

Leora shrugged and smiled. She had perfect teeth.

The Oldest Member sprang up in his svelte summer suit, which, while it did not have the flair of his winter tweeds, demonstrated that under it he was remarkably well preserved. "Please sit down, Leora, and pay no attention to rules, since you are our guest." He helped her insert her elegantly slim body into the vacant chair on the other side of him. "Will your husband be here?"

She raised one perfectly groomed eyebrow. "I certainly doubt it. We've just split up."

"Oh! I'm sorry to hear that."

"It was inevitable. Some immature people can't stand competition from spouses in the same profession." Lowering her long lashes, she added, "Are you ready?"

"For competition?" asked the Oldest Member, wrinkling his brow.

"For me."

In the paralyzed pause that followed, the Interpersonal cleared her throat and said, "What did you have in mind?"

"About fifteen to thirty minutes," said Leora.

"A quickie?" said the Interpersonal, with a hint of contempt.

"Oh well," said Leora, "if you're all in a hurry, I think I'd better talk now. I'm on a diet, so it doesn't matter that I've apparently missed lunch. There doesn't seem to be a lectern, so I'll just stand behind my chair. Shall I proceed?"

"Please do," said the Oldest Member, who had evidently recovered his aplomb along with the normal hue of his cheeks.

Leora rose gracefully and circled to the back of her chair, upon which she placed her fingers, which seemed full of stunning rings. "I am so glad to be here today, to talk to this organization of fellow professionals. I want to tell you about a theory I have formulated which needs research and which I hope you will promote. It's about August, a decidedly sinister month."

"Right on," said the Pshrink who was in debt.

"As you know, August is traditionally a slow month. Most of us take our vacations then, and whatever is pending has to be put off until September when we return. It's been observed this year that August is quite remarkably slow. In fact, people are simply not behaving normally . . ."

"They're behaving too normally this August," said the same new Pshrink.

"I stand corrected," said Leora genially. "It is abnormal when people behave normally. In August. In the first place, hardly anyone seems to be separating and divorcing . . ."

The Interpersonal raised both eyebrows.

". . . with the exception of myself," said Leora, "and oddly enough for a not inevitably friendly situation, the whole thing is being conducted with calm and consideration. I have heard of similar instances, and I tell you, colleagues, that the spread of friendliness and cooperation this August is past the bounds of statistical normality for civilized human beings. As you know, civilization is a thin and constantly cracking veneer over the animal in humanity, and I —and you, my colleagues—make a living from coping with the animal . . ."

"Animals are actually less neurotic, less violent, and more civilized than people," said the Interpersonal.

The Oldest Member, who had been staring raptly up at Leora, rapped sharply on the table. "Now see here! You know perfectly well that we do make a living the way Leora has said. And I do enjoy what you are saying, Leora, m'dear."

Leora's laugh was, of course, lovely. "It is so intelligent of you to concentrate on the important issue—about the animal in human beings, I mean. We make a living from other people's problems, and those problems, the intimate ones that are most lucrative for us, seem to be rapidly decreasing."

The Oldest Member, whose chest measurement had increased following Leora's mention of his intelligence, looked puzzled. "I know we're not busy this August, but perhaps it's just too hot and humid for people to come to our offices."

Leora bent forward, straining the fabric of her blouse. "We cannot be content with explanations that do not seek out all the possible answers to the problem. It is much worse than you think. Not only are private practitioners idle, but the statistics on crime rates show a noticeable drop. And as you know, normally crime always increases in the summer."

The Oldest Member nodded and settled back with his bifocals tilted, presumably so he would have a better view.

"Furthermore," said Leora, "I think I know what's happening. Even my lover—the one I'm going to marry after my divorce—thinks I may have something."

"Ah," said the Oldest Member.

"About the falloff in business. It has to do with sunspots—surely you've been reading the articles and can guess what's happening *there*—and with those mysterious spokes in the rings of Saturn. I suppose there might be one or two of you cognizant of recent scientific developments?"

"Indubitably," said the Interpersonal.

Leora allowed her forehead to pucker in a delightful frown. "Oh. Then I want to assure you that I do not believe in UFOs that visit Earth. I do not approve of those cults that have been built around the UFO theory. However, I suspect that the UFO belief is due to an ESP phenomenon. People are tuning into aliens from outer space, but they are interpreting the ESP data incorrectly."

"You're kidding," said the Interpersonal. "Tell us you're kidding."

Leora appeared to be grinding her perfect teeth momentarily. "I never kid. I took honors at every school I attended and I am always serious about everything I do."

"Tsk, tsk," said the Interpersonal.

"Let Leora finish," said the Oldest Member.

"Sorry about that," said the Interpersonal. "I was having an ESP spasm."

"As I was saying," continued Leora, "I am here as a serious colleague. I am trying to tell you that aliens from outer space do not need to visit Earth in silly flying saucers because they have been observing us from Saturn for years. I suspect that they are now putting into action their final plans for closing in on us and taking over. Perhaps they are tired of hiding around Saturn and need a green planet. At any rate, they have chosen August—this month—to attack us in our soft underbelly."

"With sweetness and light?" said another Pshrink.

"Precisely. I do not know what they are doing to our sun, but presumably an unknown radiation especially beamed at the northern hemisphere of Earth . . ."

"I was wondering how you would excuse the unrest in the southern," said an Eclectic whose Latin American winter vacation had been passed in jail as the result of what was referred to as a slight unrest following a revolutionary coup.

". . . where there has been an increase of lassitude and ennui."

"Is this your first summer in Manhattan?" said the Interpersonal, fanning herself with her gilt-edged fan.

Leora's smile had a frosty edge to it. "I must say that you are all delightfully participatory, but in order to put my point across, I ought not to be interrupted so many times. I came here to warn you of the danger which will be noticeable in our profession long before it becomes obvious to the general public. I believe that these aliens have begun their work this August, and as the crime rate drops and people settle disputes and personal problems amicably, the danger increases."

Leora paused and took a spectacularly deep breath. "We must take care. We must find out more. We must persuade Congress to send a manned spaceship to investigate the spokes. An *armed* spaceship. We cannot waste time. I believe the motto of the aliens to be—TODAY, AUGUST; TOMORROW, THE YEAR!"

"And to think that we thought all we had to worry about was August Angst," muttered the Interpersonal.

"August what?" said Leora.

"Angst."

"What is that?"

"Anxiety. What you're telling us we don't have enough of around us in order to make a living from. If you followed that sentence," said the Interpersonal.

"I'm glad you agree with me," said Leora.

The Oldest Member's lips had gradually been pursing tighter and tighter. Finally he opened them and expelled air. "I'm curious, Leora. Did you finish your education at ———" and he named the Institute where the Interpersonal taught.

"I never heard of it," said Leora.

"My niece didn't tell me where you went to analytic school," said the Oldest Member, ignoring the Interpersonal, who had just given him a jab in the ribs.

"What niece? *Analytic* school?"

The Oldest Member pushed his chair back against the Interpersonal, who patted him consolingly as he said, "Leora, I hate to tell you this but—"

"Say," said Leora, "isn't this the dining room where SLALP is meeting?"

"What is SLALP?" asked the Oldest Member, breathing heavily.

"The Society of Lawyers for the Advancement of the Legal Profession."

The Interpersonal stifled a giggle. "You've wandered into the lunch of the Psychoanalytic Alliance, Leora."

Leora drew back, clearly in horror. "A bunch of shrinks? Nasty, unbelieving, obstructionist, crazy shrinks? Trying to trap me!" She turned and fled through the doorway.

"I thought lawyers were supposed to be somewhat saner than Pshrinks," said the Interpersonal.

"Oh, don't underestimate anybody," said the Oldest

Member. "I've had some fascinating cases, and then there's that brother-in-law of mine."

"What lawyers are like is irrelevant," said the Pshrink in debt. "Leora had a good point."

"Two of them," said the Interpersonal mournfully.

"Isn't there a germ of truth in what she said?" asked the Oldest Member. "Aren't there newly discovered spokes in Saturn's rings?"

"Yes. The wonderful Voyager pictures showed them."

"And is there a good scientific explanation for them?"

"Not yet, but there's no reason to think that they are in any way artifacts with any connection to alien intelligence," said the Interpersonal.

"But there is the fact that patients seem to be doing fine without psychoanalysis this August."

"Yes," said the Pshrink in debt. "Pshrinks on call for other Pshrinks have nothing to do. Nobody is calling up anybody. Nobody has angst . . ."

"Except us," said the Interpersonal. "I mean all of you. I am not worried."

"Neither are any of us," said the Oldest Member. "I hear you all complaining, but you don't *look* worried. I have noticed the dearth of patients but I don't mind. Do you really mind?" he asked the Pshrink in debt.

"Now that you pin me down, I admit that I don't care. I'll just take longer paying off, and in the meantime, this is a pleasantly lazy month."

"And I'm unusually happy too," said another Pshrink. "Ordinarily August Angst affects my patients so much that I feel guilty when I take the normal August vacation, and this year I decided not to, yet I'm hardly busy and it doesn't bother me. Something must be wrong."

Suddenly the Oldest Member took off his jacket and wiped his forehead. "A horrible thought has come to me. Or possibly a hot flash. You are right. Something is wrong! If our patients are tranquil and we are complacent, and even the *lawyers* aren't busy, then the world must be in trouble."

At that moment, the door to the dining room opened again and two young people rushed in.

"Gee, we're sorry to be so late," said the young man, short and sandy-haired. "I guess we've missed lunch, but we wanted to meet you all anyway. It's an honor to be invited to a Pshrinks Anonymous meeting."

The petite young girl nodded and smoothed down her red curls. "We really couldn't help being late. Bellevue Psycho is positively jumping. Last night there were a lot of admissions, and the clinic is overloaded with applications of patients who want a substitute therapist for the summer, and if any of you are going to be working through August, would you tell us if you have time to do some consultations and take referrals?"

The Oldest Member jumped to his feet, procured an extra chair, and placed it between himself and the Interpersonal for the young girl. The couple sat down and he beamed at them. "I'm the Oldest Member of Pshrinks Anonymous. My niece said you wanted to meet me and here I am."

"Why, you're not old at all!" said the girl. She had perfect dimples.

"Do have some Regressed Rice Pudding," said the Oldest Member. "The Limeade Libido goes well with it, m'dear."

The Interpersonal sighed.

"It's just the absence of August Angst," said one of her colleagues.

"Oh?" said the Interpersonal. "Today, lawyers, and tomorrow . . . ?"

SEASONAL SPECIAL

In the middle of September, even in the subbasement dining room of the Psychoanalytic Alliance, the hay fever season is obvious, thanks to a resonantly sneezing chorus of Pshrinks.

"One of these years I'm going to spend late summer and fall in Europe. Or California. Or Mars. Anyplace where ragweed doesn't grow." From the large box she was clutching on her lap, the Interpersonal plucked another tissue and sneezed into it.

Totally unwilted by an upper respiratory problem, the waxed tips of the Oldest Member's silver moustache were as jaunty as ever.

"I," he announced smugly, "am immune to hay fever, as anyone well analyzed should be. I am ashamed that so many of the Pshrinks Anonymous are susceptible to trite and socially demeaning diseases with strong psychogenic overlay."

The Interpersonal moaned softly and poked gloomily at the Free Floating Fish lying before her.

One of the Oldest Member's much younger Freudian colleagues blew his nose in a trumpetlike bravura and said, "I'm sorry to disagree with my esteemed colleague, but an allergy is an allergy. One is genetically susceptible or not, as the case may be . . ."

"Hah!" said the Oldest Member. "Whatever my genetic heritage is, I am confident that my defenses are non-neurotic."

"I suspect," said the other Freudian, his voice rising, "that you may have forgotten—if it was known at the time you were in medical school—that it's the body's *defense* against ragweed that causes hay fever. Allergic people have too adequate defenses . . ."

"Too neurotic," said the Oldest Member, determinedly sawing away at the overdone Claustrophobic Corn Cake. "I feel secure in my opinion—which some of you may have heard me state—that mine was the only medical school worth going to, at the right time."

Other Pshrinks began to join the argument, and as the decibels rose, the Interpersonal shouted, "Wait! I know you all love to argue, but why don't you listen instead to an interesting case I saw recently. It involves allergy."

"Yours?" asked the Oldest Member.

"I suppose it does. Yes, I think my hay fever is quite responsible for the outcome."

"That I would like to hear," said the O.M.

"Spare us!" came in a loud chorus from other Pshrinks, while the various sneezers went into action, presumably due to the emotional provocation.

"Try not to break up my narrative flow with the usual hostile remarks," said the Interpersonal.

"The mucosal flow is more likely to dry up if you go home and take a decongestant," said one of the Eclectics.

"Decongestants are bad for me," said the Interpersonal, "but I am certain that attempting to tell a story under critical duress will rev up my autonomic nervous system and stimulate my adrenals so that the increase in adrenalin will enable me to breathe properly for a while."

"Let's take a vote on going home," said a sneezer.

"You wouldn't want to deprive a girl of the chance to stop sneezing for a few minutes," said the Interpersonal. "I will proceed:"

I will call this patient Uni [said the Interpersonal], which is not, of course, his name. According to the referring doctor, his wife's analyst, Uni was a ruggedly handsome, middle-aged man who retired early from an executive position after a car accident which fractured his skull. Uni was apparently somewhat odd before the accident, and more so afterward. With inherited money and an ample pension, Uni lived in a large house in a distant suburb, surrounded by trees, flowers, and weeds, all disgustingly allergenic except that Uni was not allergic, unlike some of us who have to spend the season cooped up in air-conditioned offices with ionizing filter machines going full blast . . . where was I?

"Narcissistically preoccupied with your ailment," said the O.M.

Thank you. That's part of the story. I was indeed preoccupied because on the day that I saw Uni for a consultation, the pollen count was out of sight, the wind was blowing it over from Jersey, and the humidity was too low to make the damn grains sink. I had early given up and taken what a friend had sworn was an antihistamine without noticeable side effects.

Not only was I experiencing the full force of the main side effect, paralytic somnolence, but I was getting no relief from the hay fever symptoms.

"I'm not going to come here again," Uni announced as he sat down, "because this won't help. I'm only coming *here* so no one at home will find out I'm seeing an analyst, and besides, I like to come to the planetarium occasionally. My wife's idiotic analyst thinks we're on the brink of divorce. Or maybe he thinks I'm crazy. Maybe my wife does."

"Do you?"

"I don't want to talk about it."

"Okay," I said, going on to ask basic questions about his past and present which he answered readily, while I snuffled gently into my Kleenex from time to time and felt as if I were talking underwater.

"Nasty cold you have there," said Uni after I ran down.

"Hay fever."

"Just like my wife, who says it's worse this year because I make her tense. She says if I continue to hide out in my telescope room she'll run off with her allergist, who's even younger than her shrink."

"Hiding out?"

"Not really. I've just got a room with a skylight above the couch so I can use my telescope. The weather's been so clear lately . . ."

Involuntarily, I grimaced.

"Sorry about that. Rain would take the ragweed pollen out of the air temporarily, although my wife says it increases the mold spores. Not that rain actually makes any difference to me now . . ."

He paused, a look of dismay passing over his face. Patients tend to get that look when they find themselves telling you something they hadn't intended to on the first consultation. I raised my eyebrows.

Uni massaged his chin. "I see that you are wondering, in your fiendishly clever psychoanalytic way, why rain doesn't interfere with my astronomy hobby now."

Fiendishly, I said nothing.

"If you hadn't gotten me onto the subject of allergy I wouldn't have slipped and revealed that fact. And you know that it's a pain for me to come here."

I sneezed.

"I suppose you're telling me that I'm a pain. I suppose I am. It's too bad, since I really love my wife, that I've had to upset her so much, but I couldn't very well tell her the whole truth. I suppose I ought to explain why rain doesn't bother my astronomy hobby anymore?"

I nodded.

"You see, I got interested in astronomy after my accident,

when I was laid up for a while and couldn't sleep nights. I bought a decent telescope and then I made a bigger one. I looked through them, and looked through them, and . . . well, after a while I was there all the time and my sex life dwindled to nothing and I kept on looking through the telescopes, and I studied and studied . . ."

As his voice died away, his eyes rolled to the ceiling and his lips moved silently.

"You look at the stars?" I asked, wondering if perchance he was actually studying the neighbors.

"Not anymore. In those long nights—quite dark out where I am—I concentrated hard on looking at everything in our galaxy, and then I tried to find as many other galaxies as my telescopes would let me—I spent a lot of time on that blur that's M31, when I could see it, and then I thought, and thought—beyond . . ." He died out.

"Beyond?" I asked, wondering in my antihistamine stupor which of us was going crazy.

He seemed to snap out of his. "My wife thinks I study but I go to the room—to meditate." He blushed and looked guilty.

Several minutes passed, while I attended to my leaking nose.

"I can see that you doubt my veracity," he said. "You took three tissues since my last statement, and that must have significance."

I couldn't think of anything to say, and was not sure I'd be able to say it if I had. I remembered that antihistamines sometimes had the effect of virtually depriving me of speech . . .

"Have one," said a Pshrink, holding out a pillbox.

. . . and I felt terribly guilty myself about taking one on a working day. I threw my used wad of tissue into the wastebasket and took a fresh one, possibly two. I was careful not to take three.

"Yes, yes," he said testily, "I get the point. I should throw out my theory, just as my science-fiction-reading son said I should, but what do science fiction people know? They aren't *living* it the way I am, and I can tell you that living it is much more difficult, exhausting, full of responsibility, yet glorious, glorious . . ."

He went on like this for some time while my eyes glazed over and eventually the inevitable happened. I sneezed again.

"Good. Excellent," said Uni. "You are reminding me that reality—and my wife's analyst thinks my contact with it is dim—is ever present, even in my theory, which is as much a part of the Universe as your sneeze is. Thank you for appreciating me."

At this point, in despair, I managed to bring my voice up to a slow croak. "What theory?"

"Haven't I told you? Well, you know I'm not yet a professional astronomer, able to get people to listen to billions and billions of my words; but maybe people, even you, won't want to listen, because death isn't easy to face."

Wondering if he'd brought a lethal weapon, I asked, "Whose?"

"The Universe, of course. What in hell do you think I've been talking about?"

"Um . . ."

"You mystics and your *Om!* Don't try to tie it in with steady-state and tell me the Universe won't die. Astronomers say they don't know for sure, but I know. There's enough total mass in the Universe for it to stop expanding and eventually collapse—and die." He began to cry. "In agony, perhaps."

"But . . ."

"Now don't start telling me that we'll be long gone by then and won't suffer, because I don't have a petty human perspective. I've talked to the Universe and I know the truth."

There was a long pause while I digested this, my adrenaline shooting up, so that I did not sneeze, sniffle, or fog out.

The patient leaned forward. "The Universe is alive, conscious, self-aware, and knows it's going to die!"

I took a chance and said, "*You* are alive, conscious, self-aware, and know that some day you will die. It's called the human condition."

"Damnation! I am insane! I have conversations with the Universe—don't reduce that to simple mumbling to myself about myself."

"Perhaps it's the same thing. Aren't you part of the Universe? Perhaps that's how it knows—"

Uni gasped. "You understand! Now you know the truth! I am the reason the Universe has to die!"

I was lapsing into semicoma and none of this was making sense. "You? How can your mass make the difference between continuous expansion or eventual collapse?"

"The problem is not my weight but my mind. My consciousness. Mine and yours. Don't you see that life itself, with its logical extension, intelligent life, is what causes the fatal consciousness of the Universe? In those long still nights sitting beside my telescopes, I have tuned into the Universe and I know that it started as *purity.*"

"As in no sin?"

"As in no self-awareness, no evolution, no death. That kind of purity is ruined by life."

"Well . . ."

"You're right. The Universe experiences a well of loneliness as a result of becoming alive. It was all a mistake having a Big Bang, then galaxies and complex molecules and life."

I sneezed. Then I decided not to argue with him or try to get the session back on a more analytic footing, which, thanks to hay fever, I had never quite achieved anyhow.

"Ah, you disagree," said Uni. "A sneeze is inevitable, so why not life? Clever of you. It makes me think. I have been so busy trying to soothe the Universe, showing it that I, its child, understand and share mortality." He wiped away a tear. "My thoughts are that each time one of us intelligent offspring of the Universe dies, the Universe is freshly reminded that it too will die someday. I'm afraid! It must hate us!"

"Ask it."

"Are you kidding? You probably think I'm hallucinating. I'm supposed to ask my hallucination if it's mad at me?"

"Might as well."

He sat back, closed his eyes, and his lips twitched for a while.

"That's odd," he said finally. "The Universe not only isn't angry, it laughed at me!"

"That upsets you?"

"It was a *raunchy* laugh! Maybe it likes being mortal, since the invention of sex goes along with it. Oh—my wife will be pleased. I think I've just lost my inhibition."

He looked speculatively at me and I was grateful for the disaster that hay fever inflicts on one's appearance.

"But what caused the Universe to evolve sex—and us?" said Uni. "Don't tell me to ask it because I know it won't tell."

"What do *you* think," I asked in approved Pshrinkese for once, resisting the urge to reach into my sinuses and scratch away the itchiness.

Uni stared at his shoes. "I don't know," he said with the intense anxiety of someone who always has to know.

I sneezed.

"Thank you! You're right on the mark. I'm beginning to understand. I should have thought of it before, because thanks to my wife's allergies, I know about antigen-antibody reactions. An antigen is a foreign substance that produces antibodies in the body. An antibody is part of the body's immune response, but in allergies they work overtime, and that's what happened to the Universe."

"It is?"

"You needn't be analytically provocative. I know you understand from your own intimate personal experience that it's a matter of being raped."

"What!"

"The Universe. Being raped. By an antigen, of course."

"*What* antigen!"

"Probably the dark invader."

He was not laughing, and I promptly sneezed for the umpteenth time. I'm ashamed to admit it, but I may have muttered "Oh, God" as an involuntary comment on the day's pernicious pollen count.

"It could have been a god," said Uni, his face relaxing somewhat. "I remember that the pagan gods were always raping hither and yon. Well, the basic unsullied purity of the Universe got raped by the invader . . ." He paused and frowned.

I said nothing because my throat had clogged up and I was too stunned by Uni's instantaneous leaps into the unconscious—whose, I wasn't sure.

"No, I can't carry your suggestion to the biblically appropriate conclusion," said Uni, in severe lecturing tones. "I don't like the notion that the invading antigen-god was like the serpent entering the garden of purity to rape. Perhaps the invading god simply wanted to experiment and inadvertently caused the anaphylactic response."

I may have choked at that point.

"Yes, I realize that I am verging on genius," said Uni. "The explosive allergic reaction of anaphylaxis was the Big Bang, after which the Universe settled down to the chronic allergic defense of developing antibodies, et cetera."

"Et . . ."

"That's it. They ate each other—matter, I mean. Evolution. Then the ultimate defense, intelligent life, and the worst allergic reaction—consciousness!"

I found my voice. "Are you saying that consciousness is the hay fever of the Universe?"

"Isn't that what you've been helping me to see? Now, are you going to help me find out whether or not the invader *intended* this? Was the experiment deliberate? Look how much trouble it's caused!"

While thinking of something to say, I felt a drip coming on and grabbed the tissue box. One Kleenex went to my nose, but several mysteriously flew to the carpet in assorted shapes.

"That's it!" yelled Uni. "The invading antigen wasn't an anthropomorphic god! It wasn't intending anything. It was merely a *pattern* transferred from one universe to the next, and it's up to us to see what we can do with it."

He sat back, smiling. "Well, well. Thanks to your brilliance I believe I have arrived at the obvious answer, and I think I won't have to talk to the Universe anymore. I think I'll take my wife to a marriage therapist in our town and *we'll* talk."

I smiled at him and sent silent pity to the next therapist.

Uni went to the door. He stretched and seemed to glow all over. "I feel great. We conscious creatures aren't just giving the Universe the experience of death, but the joy of being alive—even if it's all allergy. Perhaps you allergic people are more alive than others?"

I considered this. I did not swear and tear at my hair. I did not throw anything at him. I sighed. "That's an interesting theory. I'll have to think about it—after the hay fever season."

"M'dear," said the Oldest Member, "I trust you will refrain from tuning into *cosmic* allergies when the season is over."

"Um," said the Interpersonal. "I recently had skin tests for year-round molds and dust . . ."

THE BEANSTALK ANALYSIS

Strange happenings within the field of psychoanalysis are bound to surface during the weekly luncheon meetings of the Psychoanalytic Alliance, referred to by the more uninhibited as Pshrinks Anonymous because of its strict rule that members must conceal the identities not only of their patients but also of themselves. This dangerously ecumenical club meets in a fading Manhattan hotel willing to risk its reputation with dubious clientele, and has always rented a private dining room in the subbasement.

At a recent lunch, the Oldest Member—an unreconstructed Freudian—was holding forth as usual, drowning out the conversational attempts of the assembled Jungians, Adlerians, Kleinians, Ego Psychologists, and assorted other points of view.

". . . I admit that the Master himself had a daughter, but letting in women as well as these newfangled heresies . . ."

"Women and heresies are hardly new, even here," muttered one of the members grizzled with Eclectic experience.

". . . is a mistake," continued the Oldest Member, "because these newfangled so-called analysts don't do orthodox depth therapy." He scowled at an Interpersonal over his cigar, unlit because this same Interpersonal had put through a no-smoking rule.

The Interpersonal smiled and crossed her legs. "Fortunately there's room for everything at Pshrinks Anonymous,

including the right of a female member to present a case
. . ."

The Oldest Member gripped his cigar tighter and cleared
his throat ominously. "Surely I have never recounted my
series of successful cases dealing with the repressed sexual
phobia implicit in cigar aversion manifested by certain female—"

"You have," said the Interpersonal, "here and—volumi-
nously—in print. Now I am going to tell about a case that has
had to be kept not only anonymous but—you must believe
me, colleagues, unpublished."

"Unpublished!"

Even the Oldest Member was silenced.

I was just out of residency at the time [said the Interper-
sonal], renting a small office on the ground floor of an old
converted Fifth Avenue town house. I was able to afford this
prestigious address only because it was going downhill because of the long delay in completing the demolition of the
building next door. I was working my way through analytic
school, still paying off loans incurred while a psychiatric
resident, and I needed patients.

One of my sources of referral was a well-established analyst known to Bellevue resident psychiatrists as Tailored
Tweeds, who would send me patients so unsuitable for classical analysis that they could in good conscience be dumped
on a mere stripling who was not only of the wrong sex but
also of the wrong analytic persuasion.

When I took a history from my latest referral, it turned out
that T.T. had actually treated him for several months, which
meant one of two things: the patient had become too crazy
or insolvent.

"My business is doing better than ever," said Mr. K, raising his voice over the demolition noise next door, "and I've
remodeled a brownstone for my family . . ."

I sighed, and then I sneezed.

"I suppose you're allergic to cigars too," said Mr. K, who had obeyed my nonsmoking sign but still reeked of tobacco.

"Too?" I asked.

"My wife is allergic. That's why I'm in the mess I'm in."

"What mess?"

"My ex-shrink thinks I've become psychotic and said a change in therapy was indicated, preferably to the opposite sex to work out my hostility from and to my nonsmoking wife."

"Do *you* think you're psychotic?"

"Well, I hallucinate."

"What?"

"I said I—"

"I heard you. What sort of things do you hallucinate?"

"Encounters with aliens from outer space."

"Tell me about it," I said reluctantly. I am an SF addict and do not approve of fringe elements invading the field.

"My wife says I've always been boringly sane, so what's happened has been a traumatic experience, especially since I only agreed to go into analysis because my wife couldn't stand my cigars and it was affecting our sex life."

"I seem to recall that your ex-analyst smokes," I said.

"Yes. Cigars. We spent a while analyzing my wife's sexual hang-ups shown in her aversion to smoking, but for some reason this didn't help in bed."

There was a loud crash next door and the patient quivered. "I think I'm having another hallucination. I imagine that there's a crack developing in your wall in back of that avocado plant next to the fireplace."

I turned to look. "You're right—there is a crack."

"It's a pity about these old mansions," said Mr. K, staring at the crack. "This one should be saved by the Landmarks Commission. I noticed the gargoyles when I came in. Of course, if that demolition damages your building structurally you'll have to move; and then I'll have to get used to another office and—"

"I thought you came to tell me about the hallucinations connected with your cigar smoking."

"You interrupted my free association!" said Mr. K plaintively. "Do all women analysts talk a lot?"

I ground my teeth but remained silent, demonstrating that I, too, could play the classical analytic game.

After a few minutes Mr. K reached into his pocket and extracted two shiny objects resembling very large black beans. He dropped one of them into the small glass vase containing ivy that stood next to the inevitable box of Kleenex on the patient's table.

"See?" he said.

The water turned dirty gray, foamed, and quieted to reveal a heap of sediment on the bottom and wilting ivy on top.

"Now I've got only one left," said Mr. K. "Do I plant it? Is it real? Did you actually see the other bean dissolve?"

"I saw it, and my ivy is having a traumatic experience. Where did you get those beans?"

"A few nights ago I was up on the roof of our brownstone at about 3 A.M. because I couldn't sleep and that's the only place where my wife lets me smoke. I was sitting in the doorway because it was raining slightly, and my cigar went out, and there right in front of me was that damn Greek god my wife picked up during our last trip to Europe. It's a big obscene marble statue without even a fig leaf—"

"You didn't like it?"

"I hated it. That night I had persuaded my wife to let me trade it in the morning to our neighbor for a birdbath he didn't like because it attracted pigeons, but my wife's crazy about pigeons and agreed because she wanted the birdbath—"

"What happened at 3 A.M.?"

"There I was sitting in the dark, undoubtedly full of primal hostility, when this funny patch of light, like a beach ball full of energy and lit up from inside, bumbled along in the air and came to rest on the head of the statue and began to talk to me, not exactly in words, but—"

"Then how?"

"I don't know how. Meanings came into my mind but I can't remember them. The ball threw the beans at me and left, or died; anyway it wasn't there anymore."

"Is it possible that these beans were up on the roof to begin with and that you missed seeing them when you first went there?"

"You sound like my ex-shrink. If I'd seen the beans then I'd be certain I hallucinated the ball—I don't like the alternative."

"I see. The alternative is that a lighted beach ball actually talked to you."

"Yeah. You seem awfully young to handle a raving psychotic. What are you going to do for me, Doc?"

I didn't have time to tell him that I never answer that one. My intuition was working, as indicated by the tingling at the base of my spine. "I wonder if perhaps you haven't told me everything that happened," I said.

"Um. There were a lot of beans but they dissolved in the roof puddles. I rescued three before they got wet, and then I put one in a puddle to see if it would dissolve, and sure enough—"

"Isn't there something else?"

"You do interrupt a lot. Well, all right, I'll tell you, but don't laugh. That bastard of a beach ball said it wanted to make a trade for the statue, said I'd get something expensive. We sort of seemed to bargain; and I forgot all about the deal with my neighbor; and the next minute, whammo, the statue and the ball were gone and there I was with two lousy beans, a missing art object, and a hostile wife."

At that moment my doorbell rang.

"My time is up," said Mr. K, leaping for the door like an escaping prisoner or possibly a well-trained patient. "It's Friday. Can you see me for an extra session tomorrow?"

"I'm sorry, but I'm going out of town. On Monday we'll continue discussing your problems about your wife. And the beans."

"Can I leave the last bean here? Maybe I wouldn't feel so crazy if somebody else took the responsibility for a while."

I nodded. He placed the bean on the soil of the avocado plant and went out smiling.

When I returned to my office Monday morning, I arrived early, as I always do after a weekend, to see if the plants needed watering.

The avocado didn't. It wasn't there, having been replaced by something which resembled a large beanstalk. Around the pot was a residue of water, possibly all that remained of the avocado, which had been a good-sized tree. The roots of the usurping stalk emerged from Mr. K's bean but did not actually enter the soil, extending instead horizontally to infiltrate the ceramic pot itself. Then they emerged onto the marble of the fireplace hearth. When I touched a root, it seemed to be anchored to the marble.

My first patient, also early, rang the doorbell; and there was no time to do anything definitive about the beanstalk, like putting in an emergency call to the New York Botanical Garden or consulting an exorcist. A busy young psychiatrist never has time to do anything definitive about anything, but does learn to act quickly in an emergency. I took the screen from around my typewriter table and used it to conceal the fireplace and its beanstalk.

By the time Mr. K arrived for his afternoon appointment, the beanstalk was thicker, tightly wound, and reached the ceiling. The roots covered the fireplace in every direction, apparently ingesting and digesting the marble with ease.

With the screen removed, Mr. K and I surveyed the beanstalk.

"I think I'm having a traumatic experience," he said through pallid lips. "May I smoke? Please?"

"Oh, what the hell," I said. "Go ahead."

There was another crash from the demolition and the crack in the wall widened. Mr. K shuddered and lit up.

I sneezed. The beanstalk uncoiled. It was much larger than I had realized.

Mr. K puffed nervously on his cigar. I coughed. Vibrating, the beanstalk slowly bent down from the ceiling, as if searching for a way out, and suddenly the top of it dived into the fireplace. Downwards.

"It's drilling through!" cried my patient. "Tell me this isn't really happening!"

Before I could answer, he had thrown his cigar onto the beanstalk in what may have been a hostile act.

At once the plant whipped around and grabbed both Mr. K and me with lashing branches that bound us feet first to separate sections of the stalk. The tip of the plant began to tunnel rapidly into the basement below, and as the plant's leaflike structures closed around the length of the stalk— protecting us humans, perhaps incidentally—I saw from inside that the drilling tip had become an everted nose cone which thrust down and down . . .

"I trust you're not going to indulge in Freudian implications, m'dear," said one of her older colleagues.

"Oddly enough, some events seem to be indubitably Freudian," replied the Interpersonal.

While the plant—or whatever it was—grew rapidly from all the marble, brick, and cement ingested on the way to the foundations of my building, I was not able to discuss this phenomenon because one of the tendrils had wrapped around my throat, preventing me from speaking. Mr. K was not so inhibited.

"Straight into the unconscious!" he shouted. "At last, a real depth experience!" He began to chortle like a case of backward dementia or a Pshrink who is writing a scathing review of another Pshrink's book.

I tried to reply but succeeded only in gurgling.

"What? Did you ask me what I mean by that?" he said, putting words into the therapist's mouth as they all do. "I don't know. Is it a punishment nightmare? About my sexual problems with my wife? About my erotic transference to you? The effects of smoking? It's a good thing none of this is really happening because if it were, how would we get rescued?"

How, indeed? People would assume that the demolition next door had accidentally destroyed us along with my building. No one would know that an alien plant had taken two humans with it to wherever it was going. If it needed hard minerals to eat, it might go straight through the granite under Manhattan, getting bigger as it went, perhaps to revel in the hot basalt under the granite, feeding on the entire rocky part of planet Earth.

I shut my eyes against the dust. Mr. K, still talking, had switched to believing he was in a particularly symbolic dream which he proceeded to interpret in a way that would have made Freud stroke his beard thoughtfully. I do not have time to recount this interpretation, which was in any event contrary to my theoretical point of view.

Suddenly there was a tremendous vibration in the beanstalk, the forward section of which was already well beneath the foundations. The stalk coiled against itself like a spring winding up, and just before I thought I would be squeezed to death, the spring let loose, shooting Mr. K and myself back up the beanhole into my office.

Mr. K staggered onto my couch just as the demolition engineer looked through the hole where my fireplace used to be, and apologized for having, he thought, broken through our wall.

Mr. K blinked his eyes, thanked the engineer, and announced that he was cured. He said that the structural trauma to his analyst's office had miraculously freed him from his neurotic problems, which he dimly remembered as stemming from an allergy to beans.

When Mr. K sent his check in the mail some weeks later, he enclosed a note thanking me effusively for the best short-term therapy since Freud. Not only had he completely lost any desire to smoke, but his sex life had improved to the point of being outstanding.

There was profound silence in the dining room of Pshrinks Anonymous until the Oldest Member unclamped his teeth from his cigar, and said, "The speaker should not have discharged the patient from treatment, since the return-to-the-womb aspects of the problem were never analyzed but only acted out. I've always said that you can never tell what's going to happen with improper nonclassical technique . . ."

A fierce argument promptly ensued among dissident analytic sects, not for the first time at Pshrinks Anonymous. It was cut short when the youngest member spoke. He was only a first-year resident at Bellevue Psycho (there's always one as a token example of the younger generation), and therefore it was to be expected that he would not be able to concentrate on theoretical essentials.

"I'd like to know," he said, "if that plant is down chomping on the bowels of our planet right now."

The Interpersonal shook her head. "The beanstalk ran into the same problem they were having at the demolition site. The long delays were due to the fact that every time the excavators dug beneath the old foundations they ran into one of those buried streams that are found throughout Manhattan. I understand that the new building erected in that location still has times when the underground garage gets flooded."

"Then did the alien plant—"

"When I inspected the hole in our basement, I discovered that our visitor from, presumably, outer space had reached the underground stream and dissolved. Cigar smoke wasn't the only thing lethal to its physiology."

The Interpersonal smiled at the Oldest Member and added, "Soon there was no evidence left of any alien, but I defy any alienist here to describe a better case of depth analysis."

They all began to speak at once.

THE HORN OF ELFLAND

One of the Interpersonal members of the Psychoanalytic Alliance put a plastic container on the lunch table and said, "I have brought blueberries for dessert, to celebrate the Horn of Elfland faintly blowing."

Startled, the other members of Pshrinks Anonymous stopped trying to dissect Stressed Squab without spilling Primal Peas off their plates. "How did you get blueberries in midwinter?" asked a Pshrink.

"Don't you mean *horns* of elfland?" asked a literary Pshrink.

"No, she doesn't," said the Oldest Member, "and wherever you got those berries, m'dear, they will go well with those cookies I brought to thank you for giving me your Philharmonic ticket in the emergency."

"Chocolate chocolate chip!" said the Interpersonal. "Food being the music of love—"

"I disapprove of all these misquotations," said the literary Pshrink, "as well as the references to food."

"Silence!" said the Oldest Member. "I intend to tell a story about music."

"Perhaps it will be a story with Zen implications," said the Interpersonal.

"Don't be ridiculous," said the Oldest Member, staring at her with heavy suspicion.

She seemed to be meditating on a cookie. "When I'm eating, I eat. When I'm listening to music . . ."

"That will do," said the Oldest Member.

Last week [he said] I received a call from my internist, who is not only one of my oldest colleagues but someone upon whom I depend heavily, since—you will be astonished to learn this—I find it incredibly difficult to acquire a reliable authority figure at my age, much less another M.D. who isn't a complete ass. My internist doesn't quite measure up, but he's the best I know, so I'm always willing to help him out when I can. His problem was his ne'er-do-well grandson, now about thirty, who seemed to be in urgent need of psychiatric attention.

I reminded my internist that his grandson was obviously not suitable for classical Freudian analysis, my specialty, but that I would consent to doing a few emergency consultations.

When I saw the patient last Thursday morning, he proved to be a short, energetic chap with a sparse brown beard and a wild look in his eyes.

"Hullo," he said, sitting down on my couch. "I suppose Grandpops has told you his diagnosis—that I'm crazy and that I've wasted my life trying to find myself. I suppose I have—I've tried finding myself in graduate schools, business, hard labor, and what Grandpops calls idleness, but mostly I live on money left in trust for me by my other grandfather, and I pursue my three main interests—music, gourmet food, and Tolkien, not necessarily in that order."

I questioned him, to speed things up, since I wasn't doing

analysis. El, as I will call him, could play guitar and piano well enough to earn money with them, but had never tried. He was such a good cook that his one experiment with marriage had ended when his wife (a busy lawyer) complained that he was more interested in heating up the oven than her.

His obsession with Tolkien took the form of a preoccupation with *The Lord of the Rings* that was getting so out of hand it had certainly passed beyond the bounds of respectable neurosis.

El believed—believes—that Elves exist.

"Grandpops thinks it's insane," said El, waving his naked toes back and forth from his perch on my couch. Although it was already winter, he was in sandals. Perhaps he expected fur to sprout from his feet.

"It's true," continued El, "that I may have been a trifle overenthusiastic when I changed my name to Elrond—say, do you know what I'm talking about? Do you realize that I'm referring not to little pixielike creatures in silly stories, but to *Elves*, those tall, majestic, more-than-human creatures of Tolkien's masterpiece?"

"And you believe you are one of them?"

"Hell no. I just believe there's a real place, inhabited by Elves, which can be entered by transcending the boundaries of this dimension. Tolkien unconsciously divined the truth, that there's another universe, in another dimension, where Elves live, making potent music and eating beautiful food. I'll go there with the ring."

He paused and chuckled as if he knew he'd titillated me.

"Ring?"

"Tolkien was wrong, you know. It's not the sort of ring he described. It's a ring of music. True power comes from completing the sequence of proper vibrations, closing that ring and pushing us into the other dimension. I'm a little worried, however, about what it will do to Avery Fisher Hall."

I raised my eyebrows inquiringly. They always have notable effect.

"An earthquake will swallow up the building," he said, "but I'm going to the concert anyhow. All of them—Thursday, Saturday, Tuesday nights, and Friday afternoon. Something is bound to happen because they're playing Pinkton's *Seminal Seriatum.*"

"Whose what?"

"Serial music!"

"Cereal as in breakfast?" I asked. For some odd reason, food was on my mind.

"Serial music is composed in mathematical series, the major themes fitting a chosen form using a carefully constructed pattern of the twelve pitch classes of the equal tempered scale, intervals arranged in rows creating harmonic succession or hinting at harmonic possibilities that may or may not be fulfilled. The seriality of the piece may include timbre, rhythm, pitch—and Pinkton's will overdo the resonance properties of Fisher Hall."

"Oh?"

"The arrangements of lights over the stage, in particular, will no doubt respond when the serial music builds up resonance in the metal lamps, shaped like more rounded oriental brass bells. Each row of lights has a different arrangement of balanced numbers—five-seven-seven-five in the first row at the edge of the stage ceiling, four-twelve-four in the next row, three-six-three in the next, and twenty-four straight across in the last row. Similarly balanced but totally different grouped numbers of lights are in rows over the audience, but it's the hot ones over the stage that will react."

I was skeptical, to say the least. Perhaps my expression—although ordinarily I am the most poker-faced of Freudians—revealed my opinion, because El scowled and suddenly slapped his hands on his thighs.

"You might *try* to believe me! I know what I'm talking about! When I first saw Avery Fisher Hall after it was rebuilt inside a few years ago, I was fascinated by the possibilities. That's when I started attending as many concerts as I could.

I decided at first that the repetitive dahdahdah DAH in Beethoven's Fifth would produce interesting effects, or perhaps something Baroque and contrapuntal would, but no. I turned to more modern stuff, but only when the most serial of serial music was performed did I begin to be certain that eventually there would be the ideal composition to make Fisher Hall enter another dimension."

"And you expect to find superhuman beings? Perhaps your problems with your father—an unresolved Oedipus complex—and with subsequent male authorities . . ."

"Bosh," said El. Actually, that was not exactly what he said, but at lunchtime I will bowdlerize his speech a trifle.

"Have you met this Pinkton?" I asked, feeling that El was still in search of a father figure more suitable than his own father or, heaven forfend, his grandfather.

"Pinkton's a young punk of twenty-five who lives in Boston and has nothing to do with this except that he wrote it. He may be a modern musical genius but I'm sure he has no idea what his mathematical buildup of sound will do to the world."

"What do you mean, buildup?"

"That's the whole point. The particular composition to be played tonight builds up tonality and amplitude, with increasing dissonance, until the sound becomes unbearable for most people—and just at that moment it softens and a door at the side of the stage opens. In the darkness beyond there is an extra French-horn player hired for the purpose. We won't be able to see him, but suddenly we'll hear what seems to be an incredibly sweet note like the faraway sound of an Elven horn."

I don't know what made me do it. Most unanalytic. I found myself muttering, out loud, "Blow, bugle, blow . . ."

"That's right," said El, obviously pleased. "Tennyson described it perfectly. Wild echoes flying out into the auditorium, sweet and clear, as if from afar. Not a real bugle, not even a trumpet, because only the French horn of all the brasses can sound that sweet, that sad, that mellow—the whole irony of Pinkton's masterpiece."

"I don't understand."

"You wouldn't, unless you go to the concert. Remember now, the audience has been barraged with the buildup of unpleasant serial music, then reprieved, and then seduced by the offstage horn into thinking they'll be soothed and relaxed. What happens then is sheer genius. The horn immediately peaks upwards into incredible dissonance."

"I don't understand how one horn can create—"

"Remember that the rest of the orchestra, onstage, is still playing dissonantly but soft enough so the audience believes that everything's going to be harmonic and beautiful eventually. The horn offstage adds its sound as if to sweeten while joining the orchestra, but all at once it interrupts the mathematically precise configuration with another kind of dissonant note that sets teeth on edge, forcing the seriality of the music into fever. The orchestra goes wild and the whole thing ends in a blast."

"Sounds awful."

"I love it. I've heard it in Boston and Philadelphia, but none of those places has the right kind of hall. Fisher has a mysterious seriality built into the metal light fixtures."

"I still don't understand. What does that one French horn do that could possibly cause an earthquake?"

"Before it, there's an incredible buildup of tension, in people as well as in metal, and I believe the tension increases precisely because people are then deluded into expecting relief. When the horn's unexpectedly cruel dissonance occurs, that will complete the ring of powerful sound waves and electromagnetic waves and possibly psi waves, and will push us into Middle Earth or whatever the place is called in the other dimension. Possibly only with a minor earthquake."

"That will happen tonight?"

"Anytime the *Seminal Seriatum* is played in Fisher Hall.

I'm convinced that the first sign will be some electrical phenomenon, possibly a light exploding, just before the earthquake."

I was having trouble controlling my sarcasm, due perhaps to the fact that I knew his grandfather so well and had been forced to do this consultation. "I suppose you've calculated whether or not it matters if the lights in the ceiling are on or off?"

"Of course. During the concert, only certain dimmed lights are left on over the audience, but those over the musicians are bright and hot. All the lights are lit in a balanced pattern, so that if one light goes, the pattern will be upset, starting to unravel our ties to this dimension . . ."

He went on like this for some time, discoursing as well on Tolkien's brilliance in tuning himself to the universe of Middle Earth, although—said El—Tolkien had been led astray by his preoccupation with language when he should have been concentrating on the music of the Elves, a music that may be drawing us to the other dimension just as we are pushed by the dissonance in this.

I could get nowhere with any sort of regular psychiatric interview, but El did promise to return the next morning, Friday.

When he showed up, late, his depression and anxiety would have been obvious even to a non-Freudian.

"I've been too upset to eat," he said. "Perhaps I should have counted the studs."

"The *what?*"

"Studs in the stage walls and ceiling—eight in the side panels, I think six in each ceiling one. Yet perhaps they don't matter. If I start trying to include the vibration tendencies of that metal I suppose I should include the steel beams in the building proper and the metal in the chair seats, too."

"Are you trying to tell me that nothing happened?"

"Oh! I forgot about metal in eyeglasses, jewelry, dental fillings, watches—my God, watches, ticking away, disrupting the seriality of the piece subliminally! And what about battery watches like my Accutron, adding a ghost of a hum. And piano wires! Oh hell, I forgot about the metal in the stage machinery to raise and lower the piano! And kettledrums are the worst . . . what am I saying? This is crazy!"

I was glad he thought something was. I had begun to worry about an out-of-control manic excitement, an obvious diagnosis even if he had not begun to neglect his food intake, which makes it worse. I remembered that my wife had put a bag of cookies in my briefcase when I left home that morning, but to give a patient food! It is almost unthinkable for a Pshrink of my persuasion. Perhaps it would be unnecessary now that he was beginning to show a slight degree of insight into his own pathology.

"That's right!" he shouted. "I'm crazy to consider all the other kinds of metal, even the kettledrums. After all, timpani are tuned to different pitches, while those lights are in mathematical sequence like the music, each light identical to the others, the lighted ones warm and the unlighted ones cold."

"Since nothing happened last night, why do you persist in believing that something will?" I asked, rummaging in my briefcase.

"I wasn't quite accurate. What I wanted—I mean, what I expected to happen didn't. There was no earthquake. We didn't get to the other dimension, but at the height of the serial music, when the offstage horn came in with that incredibly dissonant addition to the rest of the blast, I'd swear that the wires for those three suspended microphones began to vibrate. All we need is for that inexperienced guest conductor to play the thing *right* next time. You'll see. The world will see!" El laughed maniacally.

"Have a cookie," I said.

He grabbed it. "Thanks. I seem to be hungry after all. It's

so depressing. Last night I didn't sleep, because I kept thinking that I was wrong."

"About the whole idea of Elfland?"

"Oh no. That exists. Somewhere. What I may be wrong about is the Pinkton. Maybe it won't send us to where I can hear Elvish music, and eat Elvish food."

He finished the cookie. "The right kind of food is important to adjust our physiology to higher planes of existence, and music will keep it there. Maybe by mistake Pinkton's music, if played *right*, is exactly the wrong music. I'm afraid —all those people sitting in Avery Fisher Hall with non-Elvish food in them, when I could cook them food that would be more Elvish, and listening to music that perhaps isn't Elvish—I'm afraid! So afraid!"

"Afraid of what?"

"Being sent to Mordor, of course! All in Avery Fisher Hall . . ."

"Have another cookie," I said.

"They're good cookies, but I can make them better," he said. "Did you know that I'm a fairly good gourmet cook? I've been trying new combinations of spices and other ingredients, creating food fit for Elves, but my conservative family disapproves."

"What about Mordor?"

His face creased as if he were going to cry. "During the music last night, watching the microphone wires sway, I thought all at once about what New York is like, about what the world is like, and now I fear we won't transcend the limitations of this universe and enter another, better one. Perhaps Tolkien combined the two possible other dimensions, better known in primitive thought as heaven and hell, and Mordor is hell. Perhaps we'll go there when the music succeeds."

"But—"

"Gee, Grandpops says you're a Freudian and I thought

those guys aren't supposed to keep making interrupting noises."

I said nothing. I did not tell him that I may have caught the disease from certain colleagues in the other camp. [The O.M. cocked one eyebrow at the Interpersonal.]

"Maybe," El continued, in a sadder tone, "that's why so many people walked out during the Pinkton, the last thing played. I know that Philharmonic audiences have a tendency to dribble out early to catch trains to whatever posh suburbs they came from, but this was almost a stampede. It's possible that's why the Pinkton didn't work."

"Couldn't it be that serial music is not to everyone's taste?"

"Most of it is harmonious and dull," said El, "but this Pinkton is an exception. Yet, if it does work, and—and—then Mordor! I don't think I could stand that. Yet it's so logical. Perhaps the opening to Mordor is created here in this dimension by the intricacies of carefully structured dissonance."

"That's the way it sounds," I said drily.

"You've heard Pinkton!"

"Ah no, but—"

"Then you've got to go to one of the concerts. Go tomorrow. Get a ticket from somebody, or try at the box office the last minute. Usually subscription holders who can't use their tickets call up so the box office can resell their seats. Please go. My grandfather is so angry with me. I've always been such a failure and he expects more from his family. I'd like one of his friends to be there when I prove myself." With that, he ran out of my office.

I decided that I had better go to the concert as an extreme favor to my internist. You [he nodded politely to the Interpersonal] were kind enough to give me your subscription ticket to the Friday matinee concert, and I went.

Unfortunately I was sitting in the third tier, as far up as you can get, clutching onto my slight tendency to agoraphobia, when the concert finally ended with markedly subdued clapping for the horrendous Pinkton thing. Perhaps the audience, what was left of it after the predictable exodus, was too shell-shocked to hiss.

Suddenly I saw El weaving his way through the exiting crowd, and before I realized what was happening he was up on the stage just as the conductor was taking his first bow after the Pinkton.

"Play it again!" shouted El. Then he crimsoned and ran over to the conductor to whisper in his ear. Some in the audience tittered, but did not stop their determined march out to the lobby. Talking earnestly, El wouldn't let go of the conductor's arm.

The concertmaster stepped up to the conductor's box and helped the conductor march El out to the wings. After a minute, while the applause died away completely, they came back without him. Another smattering of applause, clearly for politeness, was all the audience would give, and that was the end of the concert.

By the time I got down to the stage level—the elevators work slowly in Avery Fisher Hall and I am too old to run down all those flights of stairs—the backstage guards had taken El to Bellevue Psycho for observation.

Yes, I see by your faces that you read about it in one of the daily papers, not the *Times,* of course. El, however, gave a phony name to everyone, so that no one realized he was my patient, and my internist's grandson, who got into trouble. I had to go down to Bellevue and it wasn't until Sunday morning that he was released in my custody.

In the meantime, the Saturday-night concert went off without a hitch and without El's presence. He was chastened and depressed, and promised all of us, including his angry grandfather, that he would behave himself.

"I suppose that means I can't buy an air pistol and shoot out one of the lights when the offstage horn plays?" he asked.

He was clearly in need of long-term treatment.

After being sheltered in the bosom of his family the rest of Sunday and Monday, on Tuesday morning he came for another office visit with me. He seemed agitated again.

"I've just realized that someone must warn people with pacemakers not to listen to the *Seminal Seriatum,*" said El, still obsessed. "When the damn music is played properly—and I don't believe it has been so far—then not only will we go to Mordor, but the electronic vibrations will louse up pacemakers. At least I think so. Did you know that Grandpops has one?"

"No," I said, unaccountably troubled. My own internist—a man my age—with a pacemaker! I have always felt in my prime. Now I began to have doubts. Mordor indeed!

"And I've been wrong about the lights," said El, pulling at his beard. "I thought the hot ones over the stage were the ones that counted, but maybe the others over the audience are important, especially the first row nearest the stage—six and twenty-six and six. Do you think the rows with even numbers in the sets are more likely to be affected than the rows with odd numbers?"

It was hopeless. I could not get him to concentrate on anything but Avery Fisher Hall and Pinkton. I regretted not bringing more cookies and I was afraid that if he went through with his plan to go to the last concert, that night, he would have such a psychotic episode that he would not recover for a long time. I was completely unsuccessful in persuading him to stay home, but he did promise to sit still and leave quietly no matter what happened during and after the music was played. He, on the other hand, was remarkably successful in persuading me *not* to go, and to trust him.

It's a good thing that our Psychoanalytic Alliance luncheon was on Wednesday this week, because I felt like describing this case which has, after all, turned out well. My patient came to an early-morning session today and seemed considerably improved. He even brought me a present.

"After the concert last night I stayed up late and made these cookies," he said as he walked into the room. He seemed different—somehow taller, even handsome, certainly poised and calm. His grandfather must have revealed to him my penchant for chocolate chocolate-chip cookies.

"What happened at the concert?" I couldn't help asking. I had spent a restless night worrying about him, when I should have been reviewing the psychodynamics of the case and deciding on the appropriate psychoanalytic formulation.

"I guess I was wrong about the Pinkton," said El. "I should have known that in spite of the theoretical plausibility, in actuality it's impossible for any orchestra to play the music so perfectly that the proper resonance affects the light fixtures and sets up the conditions for entering another dimension. On top of that, the horn player was completely off last night."

There was a pause, and El shrugged. "It's funny, but the other dimension doesn't matter much anymore. Maybe I've accepted that we're all stuck in this one and I intend to make the best of it. It's odd, but while listening to the *Seriatum* I had a brilliant idea. I'm going to open a restaurant and Grandpops says he'll give me the money."

"Then . . ."

"I thought of calling it Elrond's Way, but there might be copyright difficulties, so I'll think of something else. I'll serve the gourmet recipes I invented while trying to discover Elvish food, and I'll have a music and light show every night —modern music and maybe computer graphics in color, projected on a large screen. I think I've finally found"—he winked at me—"my s—elf."

So you see, my fellow Pshrinks, that while El is still quite crazy, he has transformed some of it into a possibly worthwhile endeavor. I, for one, intend to go to his restaurant, although I doubt if I'll stay for the music. Have one of his cookies and I think you'll understand.

The Oldest Member stopped talking and passed around the bag of cookies.

"Best I ever ate," said several Pshrinks.

"Terrific," said the Interpersonal. "They go well with my blueberries."

"For someone who never gets fat," said the O.M. enviously, "you have always been notably interested in food."

"And in the endings of stories."

"I've told you how it ended."

"You don't know the rest of the story. I went to the concert last night."

"But your ticket was for Friday afternoon and you gave it to me."

"I got one at the last minute at the box office. I was curious. Your patient was wrong. Something did happen."

"All right, all right. I didn't suppose I could tell a case history without you being involved in some way," said the Oldest Member. "Tell us."

"Well," said the Interpersonal through a cookie, "I was sitting not in my regular seat in the third tier, but in the lower middle section of the orchestra seats. I could see the stage lights quite well. When the Pinkton horror was played, the offstage horn does at first sound as if it were out in Elfland, promising a ring of happiness."

"Happiness?" said the O.M. "I heard it, and as El said, the horn only tempts you to think that, just before it triggers off that God-awful cacophony in the orchestra."

The Interpersonal shook her head. "Last night when the horn player was supposed to switch to dissonance, the note cracked—French horns can do that even with the best players—and instead of a horrible clashing sound, we heard . . ."

"What?" asked the Oldest Member as the Interpersonal stopped speaking and stared into nothingness.

"Um. It was just as one of the lights in the stage ceiling winked out. I forgot to count exactly where it was, not being very mathematical, and of course the orchestra did eventually go on to finish the damn piece but it was ruined as far as the expected effect . . ."

"What happened!" shouted the Oldest Member.

"And afterward, I noticed that everyone around me looked a little paler and rather tense . . ."

"At this rate," said the Oldest Member, "I will need a pacemaker myself. If you don't tell us what happened . . ."

"Oh yes. You see, the cracked note, instead of being the one that produced the worst dissonance, did just the opposite. After what we'd been subjected to, that note sounded as if the promise of happiness had been kept. We didn't move into Elfland. It came in to us. Perhaps the horn player, fed up with Mordor, did it on purpose."

"I suppose you had an unusual experience as usual?"

The Interpersonal grinned. "I was sitting on the slope of a mountain eating sun-warmed blueberries that grew wild all around me. The little boy in front of me turned to his mother and said loudly, as soon as the music ended, 'I was on the space shuttle, having a great time and eating watermelon. I could taste it. I was *really there*. Where were you, Mommy?' "

"Now, you can't expect us to believe—"

"Fortunately his mother had slept through most of the last part of the concert, so she was able to say confidently, 'You're always imagining things too much, dear.' Everyone around me sighed, obviously with relief, and we all left Avery Fisher Hall, which was still completely intact and rooted in Manhattan."

"I suppose," said the Oldest Member with resignation, "that you're going to say food comes into it because it's a more primitive experience and what happened was some sort of right-brain activity induced by the amplification of vibrations in the electromagnetic fields of the neurons?"

"Well . . ."

"And I know what you're like. You'll insist that El's partial cure was in surrendering to his better self in response to my concern, and that I handled the case well because I was more interpersonally active."

"Um," said the Interpersonal, taking another cookie and pouring milk on her blueberries.

"And now you're probably going to pontificate about how we Pshrinks overdo the seeking out of internal pathology, as if the human mind contained only Mordor, when we should be helping the patient find in himself what's true and noble and . . ."

"Elvish?" said the Interpersonal.

"I knew it!" said the Oldest Member triumphantly.

"Well, I . . ."

"Furthermore," said the Oldest Member, scowling, "you will now undoubtedly insist on ending with some impenetrably obscure Zen remark that you think illuminates the mystery of life."

"Enjoy your blueberries," said the Interpersonal.

A PESTILENCE
OF PSYCHOANALYSTS

As usual, an undertone of argument permeated the sacred precincts of the Psychoanalytic Alliance, an exclusive luncheon club known to its intimates and its enemies as Pshrinks Anonymous. The Oldest Member was holding forth. This also was not unusual.

"I tell you again that these newfangled analysts use peculiar words that no one understands. If I hear any more about the parameters of the paradigmatic processes I'll eat my hat."

"You've got it wrong," said one of his younger Freudian colleagues who liked to keep up to date, "and you haven't got a hat anyhow."

"Furthermore," continued the Oldest Member, "I object to the pollution to which all of you have subjected the name of our club, adding a silent p to shrinks . . ."

"Perhaps it was inevitable," said one of the Interpersonals. "And even ominous," she added.

For once the Oldest Member looked pleased to be interrupted by a female and an Interpersonal (in order of annoyance).

"Ominous?" he asked.

Simultaneously, the rest of the membership groaned and bent closely over their desserts, Bananas Castrata Flambé. The Oldest Member nodded encouragingly at the Interpersonal, who grinned.

The experience I am about to reveal [said the Interpersonal] happened only recently and has been much on my mind. This vignette, while obviously clinical, is not a case, since the person who brought the problem to my attention was not a patient but a colleague I hadn't seen for years, a Pshrink I used to know when we both carried large iron keys to the locked wards of a well-known psychiatric hospital.

This colleague had always been a rather pedantic, phlegmatic man who yawned his way through analytic school some years after finishing his psychiatric residency when the rest of us were already analysts, struggling to stay afloat on the ever-increasing ocean of jargon. I recalled that this down-to-earth type had a limited vocabulary and what some of us referred to as poverty of imagination. He had, naturally, left Manhattan for some Other Place when he started his analytic practice.

I was shocked, then, to get a frantic phone call from him, begging me for a private lunch because he needed to discuss a confidential problem affecting his work. I told him my noon hour was free and he said he would bring lunch in his briefcase.

As we munched corned beef on pumpernickel in my office, I discovered that he was in town for one of the psychoanalytic conventions. Being allergic to cigar smoke, I had not yet been to the meetings; and I wondered what psychologically traumatic paper had affected my old friend.

"Listen, I remember that you're a sci-fi buff," he began.

"SF!"

"Whatever. Do you believe in that stuff about ESP and dreams that come true and mysterious extraterrestrial beings and whatnot?"

"I'm still waiting for the hard evidence."

"Well, I don't have any, but after attending this convention it seems to me that I detect—something."

"Alien influence?" I asked facetiously through my corned beef.

"How did you know? Are you part of the conspiracy?"

I began to wonder whether or not I was doing a regular psychiatric consultation after all. I swallowed the last of my sandwich and studied my colleague. While plumper and grayer than he had been, the striking change was the faint twitching of his shoulders, possibly due to muscle strain caused by his new habit of looking nervously over them.

"No," I said. "Tell me what on Earth you are talking about."

He sighed. "I never was much good with words, you know. I barely made it through analytic school because I had so much trouble mastering the vocabulary. Since then I've tried—oh, how I've tried, and then my wife . . ."

"She's in the field, as I recall," I said.

"Yes, a ———" (he named one of the more verbally agile allied fields). "She tried to help me; and so did some sympathetic colleagues, because at meetings I was a total loss. My papers were so easy to understand that nobody paid any attention to them, and I couldn't understand what anyone else was saying. Finally, after years of study and trying to catch up, I began to use and even understand some of the important words."

"The jargon."

"A pejorative word if I ever heard one," he said with a shrill laugh. "You see—I did it! I'm always doing it!"

"Using a big obscure word?"

"No! I mean, yes—a word with a *p* in it!"

"I am puzzled . . ."

"There, now you're doing it! I'm convinced that it's a disease, catching and deadly dangerous."

"Unfortunately our field is riddled with *p*'s—'psychiatry,' 'psychology,' 'psychoanalysis' . . ."

He moaned. "That's just it. That's why we're the conduits for the malevolent influence from outer space."

"The what?"

"You heard me." He bit into the untouched second half of his sandwich, eyeing me suspiciously over a fringe of buttered lettuce sticking out. My colleague was a WASP who always ate butter and lettuce with his corned beef sandwiches, which may be another reason why he had to emigrate from New York.

I decided to humor him. "Supposing there is a mysterious alien influence—how do you know it's malevolent?"

"You haven't been to a psychoanalytic convention lately, have you?"

"No."

"Then don't ask. Or maybe I should tell you. No, I'll just describe my own symptoms. It began with dreams, and don't try to analyze them the way Siggy would have."

"You know perfectly well that I'm non-Freudian. Tell me about your dreams."

"You sound just like me when I'm humoring a psychotic patient."

"Yep."

"What the hell. The dreams come every night. And they're full of words, most of which begin with p, that come to life in my head and chase each other around and threaten me. When the dreams began, I became aware of how everyone in my local psychoanalytic society talks like that. I used to feel I didn't belong, but suddenly I began to be part of the group."

"Comrades in jargon?"

"That's it. You don't know how I've been fighting it since I entered your office for lunch. Trying not to use many words beginning with p. I can feel them straining at the leash inside my skull, trying to get out, to join an invisible network throughout the terrestrial electromagnetic sphere . . ."

"Whoa!" I shouted, since his face was beginning to turn purple. "It does seem to be true that our fellow Pshrinks speak in a lot of p's. Does it matter whether they are silent or vocalized—the p's, I mean?"

"I don't think so, but the vocalized seem worse. 'Proclivities' instead of 'tendencies,' 'parsimonious instead of 'stingy,' 'paranoid' instead of 'suspicious,' and of course the multitude of words beginning with the unvocalized p in 'psycho.' "

"You'll have to blame most of the problem on the ancient Greeks."

He frowned. "Maybe they were subject to alien influence first. Come to think of it, maybe you're one of the ringleaders. You've got several p's in your name. The world is full of pee—"

As his voice rose in a wail, I interrupted. "You can always go to a Freudian and have your urethral complex analyzed."

"P-U!" murmured one of the club's pundits.

My highly disturbed colleague gulped and began again, in a whisper. "It's much worse out where I live and work."

"Cheer up," I said, "around here they're into illusory others and imaging and identifications that are introjective . . ."

"But where you have introjective you also have projective!"

"At least that gets us off the excretory system and onto more interesting anatomical analogies," said one of the Eclectics.

"Now let's not get carried away," I admonished him. "The world is full of people who don't use words beginning with *p*."

"Is it? My son came home from college asking me to define the parameters of a meaningful marital pairing. My daughter at medical school heard a lecture on probability factors in the success of paternal participation in parturition. When I complained to my wife that the passion was going out of our partnership, she said I was predictably puerile. Then I started having repetitive dreams of being surrounded by a posse of parameters with pink faces and pallid tongues, or possibly the other way around."

"Well, I agree with you that all these *p*'s do get to be pretentious, pompous, ponderous, and pedantic," I said.

"Pshaw! You've got it too."

"How can any of us help it?" I said, hoping that if I got into the spirit of the thing he might start analyzing me and stop being so crazy himself. "Sometimes I think that the patients have it much worse than the Pshrinks. Why just the other day—"

"You're right. Nobody says anything simply, anymore. Even patients postulate prohibitive propositions like trying to persuade me to cure their passive aggressive personality with psychodrama or their psychosomatic punishment with positioning patterns. They say they want profound sex and peak experiences . . ."

"I think I may be having one now," snarled a Freudian.

". . . and I ask you, isn't it likely that we Pshrinks are the most likely to be affected by all these p's? Day after day we listen to the voices of the people, talking and talking and talking . . ."

"Which accounts for why we tend to get verbal diarrhea when let loose from our offices," I said, proud that I had managed a sentence with no p in it.

He was not amused. "Just last week one of my patients complained about the propinquity of the couch to my chair."

"Perish forbid," I said without thinking.

"Where did you get that expression!"

"My father used to say it when he wasn't actually swearing."

"Aha! You see! Unto the fourth generation!"

"If you go back that far they weren't speaking English."

"I was speaking metaphorically, implying that the alien influence began a long time ago," he said, picking crumbs off his pants. "My theory is that if you think and speak often enough and hard enough in words containing prominent p's, your mind jells up and gets petrified."

"Paralyzed by p's?" It was impossible to resist.

He glared at me. "You are then locked into an alien mind somewhere in the universe—maybe in outer space, maybe hiding somewhere in our solar system. I don't like what could be developing in the middle layers of Jupiter, or under the ice cover of Europa."

Since his voice was rising again, I said, "So what?"

"Idiot! Don't you understand that after the aliens have gotten enough human minds locked to their system, they'll take control—take over Earth civilization!"

"I think you are—you should excuse the expression—projecting. Haven't you been worried about how the lunatic elements are trying to take over our field? I seem to remember now that you wrote a scathing paper on fringe groups."

"A paper that psychoanalysts and psychiatrists and psychologists perused without perceiving the profundity of the principles!"

"Hey! You have it bad, don't you!"

He burst into tears and threw himself prone on my couch. The afternoon sun streaming into the window made the room warm, and I was too bemused by the problem to turn on the air conditioner. My next hour, I tardily recalled, was also free, since the patient was a young psychoanalyst in training who was at that moment delivering a paper at the same convention from which my friend was playing hookey. Soon my colleague was snoring and I was drowsy enough to have a hypnagogic hallucination . . .

"You mean you fell asleep," said another Interpersonal.

"I did not," she said.

I had a momentary impression of strange lines of force from far away, converging on my snoring colleague and then transferring to me. It was rather eerie, and I was glad when he woke up and bounded off the couch.

"You're marvelous! I'm cured!" He bent down, hugged me, grabbed his briefcase, and made for the door, where he paused. "It's all clear to me. I just had to tell someone about it in order to feel OK. I guess I was only a carrier."

"You perfidious proselytizer!" I exclaimed.

"Sorry about that. I'm going home. Maybe I'll see you at next year's convention." He held up two fingers. "Live long."

"And prosper peacefully," I said as he left.

A pregnant silence ensued around the luncheon table when the Interpersonal finished speaking.

Suddenly and simultaneously some of the more argumentative members of the club began to talk.

"The parameters of the problem are . . ."

"The physiological principles in pronouncing the p . . ."

"You Interpersonals and your parataxic distortions . . ."

"And your participant observation . . ."

"Prostituting the precepts of psychoanalytical . . ."

"Perseverating in the problem of the p . . ."

"Perhaps it's only a problem of psychic phenomena . . ."

"Probably poisoned by polypramasy . . ."

"The proposition is positively polymorphically perverse . . ."

And just as suddenly they all shut up. There was an uncomfortable shuffling of feet under the table. Then the youngest member, a first-year psychiatric resident allowed in to learn from his superiors, spoke timidly.

"Perhaps it's the fault of philosophers. I almost majored in philosophy in college, and it seems to me that they promote a plethora of phrases—" He stopped abruptly, eyes wide.

"Piffle," said the Oldest Member. "None of the jargon is absolutely necessary, although I'm partial to 'id' myself."

"Would you willingly give up 'penis envy'?" asked the Interpersonal.

"I think you should keep it in your prefrontal cortex," said the Oldest Member with frosty dignity as he stroked the erect waxed tips of his silver moustache, "that I do not need to have penis envy. Nor did the Master—"

"Who was primarily a physicalistic psychobiologist," said one of the more militant non-Freudians.

"But the Master had no p's in his name," said the Interpersonal, favoring the Oldest Member's moustache with a glance of unalloyed admiration.

"Thank you," said the Oldest Member, patting the Interpersonal on the patella. "You do think that hypothesis about aliens is a lot of stuff and nonsense, don't you?"

The Interpersonal shrugged. "I haven't the slightest idea. I wish, however, that I didn't have this insatiable desire to go home and read *The Pickwick Papers*—or possibly promulgate a parody."

CONSTERNATION AND EMPIRE

"Who's the handsome stranger?" whispered the Interpersonal to her left-hand neighbor at the luncheon meeting of Pshrinks Anonymous. "Or is he a new member voted in while I was driving my husband around the lecture circuit last month?"

"I can't remember," said the Oldest Member. "The food today is so bad it's affecting what brain I've got left. Maybe he's married to that pretty Eclectic we admitted to membership recently. He's sitting next to her and—"

"No. I've just recalled that her husband is a redheaded urologist," said the Interpersonal, examining a strange length of miniature frankfurter floating in her Split Pea Soup Satyriasis.

The young, well-built, exceptionally tall stranger had a thick head of hair, unlined black skin, and horn-rimmed glasses, and was politely struggling to finish his soup.

"Nonmembers are against the rules of the Psychoanalytic Alliance," muttered the Oldest Member. "If they are present, how can we satisfy our repressed impulses toward narcissistic verbal diarrhea—after listening selflessly to other people talk all day long—and even more important, how can we complain about the terrible food?"

Since a mutter in the Oldest Member's resonant bass was equivalent to a shout from anyone else, the pretty Eclectic turned to him and said, "I'm sorry. I should have asked permission to bring my brother to lunch. He's in town for a short seminar and he's got an interesting problem case I thought needed a totally new supervisory opinion from genuine psychoanalytic experts."

The Oldest Member's brow unfurrowed, the other Pshrinks murmured assent with appropriately shy modesty, and at that moment the main course arrived.

"My God, what's that?" asked a Jungian.

"Vicious Veal Vader with Obsessive Obi Olives," read a Pshrink from the one crumpled menu.

"Left over from an SF fan club's dinner, no doubt," said the Interpersonal.

"Chef's been going to the flicks?" said one of the younger Pshrinks who was into movies as an art form.

"He believes in the Force," said one of the waiters.

"I knew it!" said the Oldest Member after the waiters disappeared. "That confounded series of science fiction movies is driving everyone crazier. It's just as well we have a stranger in our midst to take our minds off the food and onto clinical problems. What's yours?"

The stranger grinned. "By an unfortunate coincidence, my clinical case concerns just that series of films. I'm a Pshrink, too—from another city. I will preserve your club rules and remain anonymous, but for the sake of convenience, call me Luke. May I tell you about my patient—anonymously, of course?"

"Bah!" said the Oldest Member. "I don't know whether I can stand it. I have seen the films—are there three or four episodes now?—only because my grandchildren insisted, and although I found them moderately amusing, even exciting, I will probably be long gone by the time the series is complete, when the rest of you will be rich from treating the resulting mass hysterical syndromes of belief in the Force. If Hollywood's going to go whooping into the future like that, they should take Freud along."

"Judging from the oedipal implications of the second episode, they have," said another Freudian.

"I'm not at all sure we ought to waste our time talking about silly movies," said an Existential analyst who was fingering a slim volume of verse that bore his name and from which he had not yet had a chance to read aloud.

The waiters reappeared at a trot with dessert dishes which they plunked down on the table, presumably as an inducement for the assembled Pshrinks to hurry up with the veal.

"What could this dessert be?" asked a Kleinian, poking his spoon at a quivering mass.

"Probably Primary Process Psi Pudding," said the Interpersonal.

"Now you cut that out!" said the Oldest Member, who promptly turned to Luke and said, "we apologize for this uninspiring meal. I suppose you might as well enlighten us about the parameters of your problem. I mean, tell us the story."

I will call this patient Mr. C [said Luke] because lately he's been comparing himself to the movie robot C-3PO. Mr. C is a scientist who began analysis with me four years ago because in spite of his happiness in his marriage, he felt insecure about his profession and worried about his possibilities for advancement. He brooded about his inadequacies and was reluctant to write up his theoretical ideas. Socially timid in college, he had been briefly hospitalized then after becoming severely depressed when his first girlfriend rejected him. When he got into graduate school and later married, his depression seemed to have been permanently cured, but his development as a scientist was rather slow.

He and I hit it off well in analysis, although he was at least ten years older than I. He even went through the usual brief early stage of imagining me to be an all-wise authority figure, but by this year he seemed to be in the later stages of analysis, when the patient begins to see the analyst more realistically and know that he or she is not a powerful authority to be leaned on forever.

We worked hard for those four years. Mr. C now has a full-time job as a professor and has written many important papers. I thought of him as one of my more successful cases until they started showing those SF films in round-the-clock marathon sessions. Mr. C began to spend all his spare time at the theater.

Once he arrived at my office in a state of great excitement, red-eyed from watching the original Luke's adventures all night. "It's a psi experience," he exclaimed. "The Force! I can't stop thinking about it—in every sense of the word."

I assumed that this ordinarily down-to-earth patient was not getting mystical. "Force as in physics?" I asked.

"That's right. My field. I'm seething with ideas about force, but they need germination. I can't talk about them with anyone."

"Okay," I said. This was nothing new.

He switched to talking about problems connected with finding time for sex when there's a small child in the house who won't go to sleep early.

"Time for sex?" I asked. "Haven't you been at the movies every night?"

He looked wounded and I felt countertransferential. "You don't understand," he said. "It's important to go back again and again, immersing myself in the blessed simplemindedness of Hollywood that glows with Technicolor and deafens with stereophonic sound—I tell you it knocks out my inhibitingly rational left cortex so that my creatively talented right cortex can play with the concept of force. I'm getting some-where—I know it!"

"Creatively?"

"I'm going to make a scientific breakthrough at last—I'll be famous and . . . and . . ."

I waited several minutes after his voice died away but he merely gulped and looked anxious. "You don't want to be famous?" I ventured.

"I've never asked myself that question," he said. "Damned if I know the answer."

"Well . . ."

"All right—all right! I think I know. I do want to be famous, very famous—but only for something—well, good."

"Your breakthrough, whatever it is, may be good?"

"Hell yes. When it comes, I'll explain it to you—and to the whole world."

"Why can't you explain at least something about it now?"

"Because I must make absolutely certain . . ."

"Of what?"

"Of goodness." He smiled. "Now don't try to analyze this as my resistance to success, Luke."

"What do you mean? Who is Luke?"

"That's you. Haven't you seen the movies?"

From that session on, Mr. C became more resistive. He denied any fear of success, and instead described fantasies of winning the Nobel Prize for science. His persistence in call-ing me "Luke" forced me to confront him.

"Do you refer to me as 'Luke' because you're trying to deny your fear of me as a possibly malign authority figure? In those films there's a powerful, wicked character dressed in mysterious black . . ."

Mr. C burst into loud laughter. He, by the way, is white. Suddenly I realized that he was tremendously relieved, and I managed to shut up about my theory and listen to his.

"I'm close to the answer, Luke. Soon I'll be able to prove to the world that I'm right, with unassailable mathematics. I want to tell you all about it very soon. It's got to do with lines of force extending, expanding—I suppose my thinking wasn't just triggered off by those films, because the important part of the theory is the aspect of continuing, and that thought started with the birth of my son, a continuing of me, in a way. You needn't go into heavy analysis of that because it's not so neurotic. Neither is the fundamental problem of cosmological physics I'm working on."

"Then I'm not the authority figure . . ."

"No, Newton is. It's too bad that poor old Newton wouldn't have understood me either, although he whomped up the basic idea in his second law."

I was still mystified. Newton's second law is, as you all remember [the Oldest Member tugged morosely at his left moustache], $F = MA$, but Mr. C would not explain how this related to whatever fundamental problem of cosmological physics he was into.

I dug into my intuition. "You don't imagine that Newton's F is the same as the Force in those movies, do you?"

Mr. C chuckled. "You're learning, Luke, you're learning." Evading my more analytic questions, he described at length both the altered state of consciousness he'd achieved the night before in the theater, and the complaints of his deprived wife. He seemed uncommonly cheerful and left on a clear high, still calling me Luke.

The very next time he walked into my office looking like gloom frozen over, so depressed he could barely talk. His head sagged, his voice was dull and slow, and the first thing he said was

"Did you know that a dyne of force will cause one gram of mass to accelerate one centimeter per second?"

"That's first-year physics, isn't it?"

He nodded glumly, and did not answer any more of my questions until I came up with "Do you believe you've found a realistic answer for the psi powers exhibited by the characters in the films?"

"Huh?" he said, with obvious astonishment.

I repeated it, but he seemed bewildered, so I tried again. "Are you working on the idea that you can measure what they call 'the Force' in the films?"

"Perhaps."

"I suppose if you could demonstrate the reality of the Force, then everyone could have those powers of moving solid objects through air—telekinesis as good as Luke's . . ."

"Telewhat?"

Since I had been trying valiantly to make contact with the patient by entering the same ball game, so to speak, I was annoyed and explained about the movie Luke's accomplishments with psi talents.

"Oh, that," said Mr. C. "Sure. Don't worry about anything, Luke. I like you and wouldn't want to make you worry. I'll be glad to consider telekinesis for you. Perhaps it's simply a tuning in to the force of expansion so that gravity is overcome. How about that? Good enough for an SF story?"

"I wasn't really that interested in telekinesis," I said, "I wanted to find out why you seem depressed today."

"Don't worry about it, Luke. Play with something else. Does Hollywood, for instance, believe that the Force is a manifestation of God? And that gravity is the Devil? Or maybe it's the other way around. We could make a scenario out of that, couldn't we, young Luke?"

I tried to intervene, but he was off and running into free associations I couldn't follow and had no success in interrupting. Soon he was playing out loud with equations that would have been beyond me even if I still remembered differential calculus. The analysis was out of control and I couldn't get back to our previous level of mutual work on his ordinary psychological problems.

Mr. C's gloom persisted into subsequent sessions and it took me much too long to catch onto the fact that he was talking about psi factors and the movie Force merely to entertain me, as if he were trying to protect me from something. Finally, I asked him about it.

"No point in depressing both of us."

In desperation, I started to guess again. "What is it? Do you wish I possessed the powers of the film character, Luke?"

"It wouldn't help."

"What do you mean?"

"Doesn't matter. Nothing matters."

"Why?"

"Nothing matters—is a literally true statement. I might as well give up."

"Give up trying to solve your theoretical problem?"

"Oh no. I've solved that."

"You have!"

"Why the hell do you think I'm depressed?"

"I don't know. You haven't told me."

"Well, that's why. I solved it. I know the answer." He put his head in his hands and groaned. "I suppose I should say I'm ready to give up—everything. Living. Because I've given up hope."

Was he suicidal? Should I hospitalize him as he had been in college? Should I medicate him? I remained silent, turning over these possibilities in my mind.

"Don't worry, Luke," said Mr. C, as if he'd been reading my mind. "I'm not going to do away with myself, and I'm not crazy. I don't even believe in crazy things like devils—" he grunted. "The Devil. Mephistopheles. Right initial, anyway. Maybe it is."

"Please explain what you're talking about!"

"Can't burden anyone."

"Anyone in particular—besides me—that you're afraid to burden?"

"You're too damn smart, Luke. You know. It's my son. So young. Will he go crazy when he finds out the truth? Eventually somebody else will discover it, and probably in my son's lifetime."

"Truth? About what? Your previous depressive episode occurred when your girl rejected you. Do you feel rejected now, by anyone, for any reason?"

"Yes! The damn universe!"

"But . . ."

"I know, I'm part of the universe and therefore I can't be rejected and dammitall I didn't mind finding out when I was a kid that I was as mortal as anyone else and that everyone dies, and finding out later that I had to come to terms with everything ending, even a romantic dream, but I guess I always thought there was an out. Well, there isn't. And that's all I'm going to say on this damn subject."

And it was. He left my office early, saying that he didn't know whether or not he'd ever be back. There's a session scheduled for the day after I return home, but I doubt if he'll show up unless I call and tell him to come in. And if he won't tell me what he's depressed about, and I can't figure it out—what's going to happen?"

When Luke finished speaking, there was a surreptitious scraping noise as legs were recrossed and alternate elbows leaned on.

Everyone looked depressed.

"Like the food today, that case history was not calculated to uplift the spirits," said an Eclectic sourly.

"I'm sorry," said Luke, "but I think I need help. I'm afraid that if this man's depression gets worse he may actually quit work."

"Are you afraid he'll quit life?" asked the Oldest Member.

Luke took a deep breath and let it out slowly. "I know that no Pshrink can be certain about these things, but I've known Mr. C for four years and I have to say no. Besides, he's too devoted to his wife and child to commit suicide, which often is, as you know, a hostile act aimed at other people who are supposed to suffer for what you do to yourself."

"Are you afraid Mr. C will never fulfill his ambition of making a contribution to humanity?" asked the Existentialist.

"I'm sure he thinks he won't now."

"It sounds," said the Interpersonal, "as if Mr. C thinks he's making a contribution by shutting up."

"Yes," said Luke, "and somehow I've failed him. I should be able to figure out why he's depressed."

"It's quite simple," said the Oldest Member kindly. "Your patient is afraid that his wife will reject him in favor of her child. In fact, since it's difficult finding time for sex with an active child on the premises, it could be said that rejection is already taking place, bottling up Mr. C's libido. This man is suffering from the oedipal effects of having a son."

"How about the wife?" asked the Interpersonal. "Isn't she suffering sexual deprivation also? How does that fit with your oedipal theory? And wouldn't a daughter be just as much in the way?"

"Daughters," said the Oldest Member with a fondly reminiscent gleam in his eye, "are another matter—for fathers."

"Now let's not get into a classical argument," said a Pshrink who did family therapy in addition to analysis. "We're not helping Luke here."

"I think some other psychic trauma is involved," said Luke, "because Mr. C went on to say that while mystics ask if you can have a sound when there's no one there to hear it, physicists should ask whether or not you can have a force if there's nothing to exert it."

"That proves your patient is worried about God, not sex," said Luke's sister.

"Maybe, but he also said that in order for a force to be exerted, a natural field has to exist. At least I think I heard him say 'natural.' Perhaps Mr. C has been working on unified field theory."

The Oldest Member sighed. "I don't understand any of that. In fact, I find all of modern physics to be not only difficult but depressing. I liked the old Newtonian physics in which all problems seemed solvable—everything either moves or is at rest, energy is in known quantities—as we say in my trade, a little libido lost here or conserved there. So neat. The Newtonian universe was pleasant, placid, and predictable. Of course, I liked the universe best when I could believe it neither began or ended . . ."

"I think Mr. C might agree with you on that," said Luke.

"A clue!" shouted the Interpersonal, leaping up from her chair. "I'll be right back." She ran from the room as if pursued by eighteenth-century devils.

The Oldest Member raised his bushy silver eyebrows. "You can never tell what a menopausal female will do."

"But what's the clue?" asked Luke's sister.

"Pass the after-dinner mints," said the Oldest Member firmly.

"I'm afraid they're stale," she said.

"I don't care."

Luke shrugged and ate his pudding. The other Pshrinks looked dolefully at their watches. The Oldest Member munched mints.

"No," said the Oldest Member at last. "I try to keep up with modern science, but I disapprove of the indefiniteness, the appalling uncertainty . . ."

"That's why you're an antediluvian Freudian in theory even if you're a hotshot clinician in practice," said the Interpersonal, slipping back into the dining room.

"And you *like* uncertainty?" asked the Oldest Member.

"Happiness," said the Interpersonal, "is said to exist when you like what you get, not when you get what you like."

"And uncertainty . . ."

"Is what we get."

The Oldest Member frowned. "Then what were you doing outside the room—having a hot flash?"

"No—calling my husband. He understands physics better than I do. He confirmed my idea—if you rearrange Newton's equation, you get $M = F/A$."

"So?"

"Maybe Luke's patient has been working on Newton's equation, rearranged that way. Maybe he thinks—either realistically through genuine mathematics or mystically through the psychic effects of an overdose of filmed SF—that he's the first person to discover how to calculate the true quantity of force!"

Blank stares greeted her last remark.

The Oldest Member, twisting one of the waxed tips of his moustache, said, "I admit that in spite of being female and non-Freudian, you have always been reasonably sane, but am I to understand that you think Luke's patient has calculated the mysterious Force of those films?"

"I don't know whether even Mr. C would call his force the very same as that Force, since who knows what Hollywood had in mind besides making money. I think Mr. C means the force of expansion," said the Interpersonal.

"Of the universe?" asked Luke, his eyes widening.

"I see that rings a bell," said the Interpersonal.

"Yes, I think I get what you're driving at," said Luke. "No wonder Mr. C is depressed, given the sort of conscientious, humanitarian person he is. And that aspect of mortality must seem to him like a final rejection."

"Most men displaced by sons become preoccupied with mortality," persevered the Oldest Member.

"Perhaps," said the Interpersonal gently, "but what may be more upsetting to Mr. C is the inevitable death of what one loves, especially people and things one counts on to continue one in some sense."

"Ah. I see," said the Oldest Member. "Is that what he meant by 'continuing'?"

"And," said the Interpersonal, "perhaps he thought he could prove that death would not conquer *everything*. This would explain his manicky enthusiasm when he was going to the films and working on his theory."

"Which has backfired on him," said Luke.

"But what has your patient actually discovered and how?" wailed a Pshrink whose frustration tolerance had apparently come to a boil.

The Interpersonal raised her eyebrows. "The implications of being able to measure the F in M = F/A are obvious."

The Oldest Member glared at her. "I may spank you— with Great Force!"

"M = F/A means that you can discover M if you know the other side of the equation," said the Interpersonal. "The rate of expansion of the universe is known, subject to some argumentation, and if Mr. C has figured out the amount of force—"

"Whoa!" shouted the Oldest Member. "What Force?"

"The one behind the Big Bang, I assume."

"That must be right," said Luke excitedly. "Mr. C was saying something about measuring the beginning, and I now realize he must have meant that measuring the force of expansion is equivalent to knowing the force of the original explosion."

"I still don't see why he's depressed," said Luke's sister.

"Because of M," said the Interpersonal.

"M is for the many things she gave me," sang one of the more waggish Ego Psychologists, who was promptly shushed by the assembled Pshrinks.

"Maybe you're right," said the Interpersonal with a laugh, "for M *is* like mother. If A is the acceleration of expansion of the universe, and F is the force of the expansion, then M is the mass of the universe, the mother of us all. Poor Mr. C. He must have thought he was going to prove that M is below critical, but when he calculated F, M turned out to be otherwise."

"Maybe that's clear to *you*," the Oldest Member began.

"I can explain," said Luke, his eyes glowing. "To Mr. C,

real 'continuing' meant that the universe would keep expanding. He probably thought there'd be some way of avoiding the heat death when the infinitely expanding universe dies out in increasing entropy, but possibly he was just looking forward to a much longer time for life to continue."

"If M is big enough," said the Interpersonal as the Oldest Member began to chew on his moustache, "the expansion of the universe will stop. Eventually the universe will collapse."

"And everything will die," said the Existentialist mournfully, clutching his book of poems. "Even critics," he said, brightening up.

Luke nodded. "I've got to help reconcile Mr. C to the fact —if his equations are right and it *is* a fact—that the death of the universe is inevitable."

There was silence for a moment in the dim dining room of the Psychoanalytic Alliance. The Pshrinks stared down at their empty plates and sighed.

Suddenly the Oldest Member sat upright, scowling fiercely past his now limp moustache. "See here! You've got to reassure that patient—I know it isn't strict analytic technique but it's necessary—about one psychological certainty. Humanity is *not* going to go insane if he publishes his work. The capacity for denial is almost infinite in human beings. I, for one, do not intend to let the universe worry me. I have to worry about the small forces in each human life I see— including my own."

Chairs were pushed back and murmurs rose as the club members did.

"Got to remind my wife to make those plans for our trip to Alaska in the wildflower season . . ."

"I'm speaking to my agent this afternoon about promotion for my book . . ."

"I won't put off that teaching job any longer—I think I have something to offer . . ."

"Did you notice that item in the paper about a possible cure for Dutch elm disease . . ."

In animated groups, the other Pshrinks left, talking furiously.

The young Eclectic and her brother remained with the Interpersonal and the Oldest Member. The mints were all gone.

"I still don't know why I'm 'Luke' to Mr. C," said the visitor.

The Interpersonal answered slowly. "I confess that I've been to all those films, and I like them, even if I do have to wear earplugs throughout due to the decibel level. Therefore I can hazard a guess. Mr. C claims to see himself as a dithering, doubting robot but perhaps he has a secret self-image. If he calls you 'Luke' because you're young and don't understand a fundamental cosmological issue—then isn't he likely to want to be your *teacher?*"

"I'd better ask Mr. C if his ears are growing," said Luke happily.

"Never forget," said the Oldest Member, with a wink at the Interpersonal, "that no matter what our theoretical differences are, in the long run our patients become our teachers."

"Exactly," said the Interpersonal.

"I sympathize with Mr. C," said the Oldest Member. "I don't like being taught that the universe will definitely collapse. One can't quite believe that all's well that *ends.*"

"Wait!" said the Interpersonal. "Modern physics can give an out. Luke, try telling your patient—no, try asking your patient if he's positive that there has to be complete certainty about the end—or the beginning—any beginning, even the next one."

"What do you mean?"

"Your patient risked uncertainty. He took a chance—in having a son, in giving birth to a theory. How does he, or

anyone else, know for sure whether or not the universe
might not give birth to another?"

"That's a thought. He and I could talk about the universe
having a baby!"

"It's fun," said the Interpersonal, "thinking that even a
certainty has its uncertainties."

The Interpersonal and the Oldest Member strolled up-
town, arm in arm.

"I feel like an old fogey," he said. "I'd never have figured
that out to help Luke. I'm an ignoramus."

"Nonsense," she said. "You're the last person I'd ever
think of as a spent Force."

THE NOODGE FACTOR

The Interpersonal had just committed the unpardonable sin
of recommending that the Oldest Member of Pshrinks
Anonymous be more prudent in his diet and abstemious in
his smoking. A hush fell in the hallowed dining room fre-
quented once a week by the Psychoanalytic Alliance, whose
members were not noted for promoting low-cholesterol
meals or giving up their Freudian trademark of a cigar
whether they were Freudian or not.

"I happen to like Lascivious Lobster, even if the butter
sauce is calorific," muttered one of the Eclectics.

"She'll noodge you next," said the Adlerian next to him,
pointing at the Interpersonal.

"Speaking of noodging," said the Oldest Member, delicately removing butter sauce from his silver moustache and showing no signs that anything had shaken either his aplomb or his devotion to atherosclerosis-enhancing food. "Does anyone believe that the proper translation of the word is just 'nagging'?"

"I am not a nag. I am a noodge," said the Interpersonal. "Ask my husband."

"Nags are WASPs," said another Freudian. "Isn't that what you—"

"That's not the point," said the Interpersonal. "I am supposed to have cultivated noodging to a fine art, but I'm sure it's not the same as nagging. Isn't noodging more constructive, I hope?"

The Oldest Member drew out his cigar from his breast pocket, while the others gasped at the flagrant violation of the nonsmoking rule instituted by the Interpersonal. He sniffed it voluptuously and passed it under the Interpersonal's nose.

She nodded. "Why does it smell so rotten when smoked?"

"I don't know. It tastes good—to me—but I confess I can't stand the smell of *other* people's cigars," said the Oldest Member, smiling at her. "And I will try to eat more fruits and vegetables, m'dear. In the meantime, the subject of noodging reminds me of a case I am currently treating. He happens to be obsessed with the subject, as indeed most of the Pshrinks Anonymous seem to be, a good percentage of us having had Jewish mothers."

"I assure you," said the Interpersonal, "that one doesn't have to be Jewish to have been exposed to noodging, although the WASP variety usually comes disguised, in sentences beginning with 'Don't you think you ought to' or 'Wouldn't it be nice if you.' That sort of noodging has to be learned while toddling."

"You poor thing," said the Oldest Member. "I'm glad I grew up surrounded by *obvious* supernoodges. You happen to run my wife and mother a poor race, and my older brother is almost as bad. Ah well, perhaps it accounts for the splendid overachieving of so many Jewish males." He expanded his chest and twirled the end of his moustache.

"Yes indeed," said the Interpersonal, running her finger along the elegant tweed of his sleeve. "Was—is—your patient . . ."

"Successful. Very. And disturbed. Now eat your nice lobster and listen."

Mr. N, as I will call him [said the Oldest Member], had clearly been the noodgee with his mother, older sister, and wife, but at work—and he does very important work I can't tell you about except to say that it involves our country's future—he is obviously an expert noodge, mainly, I suspect, because in spite of his position of power, he never thinks he has enough power to accomplish what has to be done. He himself does not even know he's a noodge, but I do—he noodges me about the decor of my office, and the bill, and . . .

Well, Mr. N can probe and pick and shove with the best of them. He has to, because he is not in the creative end of his work, although because of him the creative work gets done.

I regret to tell this supposedly liberal-minded group that lately Mr. N's mental agitation has been definitely fueled by the new crisis over the Equal Rights Amendment. He is opposed to it, like all males who are clear-thinking . . .

"And self-serving," said one of his Freudian colleagues, reaching into her purse for a peppermint, presumably as a digestive aid, while exchanging a companionable grimace with the Interpersonal.

. . . about issues that belong to some previous century, [continued the Oldest Member triumphantly] and he complained excessively about the devotion of his wife and daughters to the cause. He was deeply depressed and I began to wonder if he didn't have a more bizarre notion developing in his rightist and righteous skull. Mind you, I like this patient, as much as anyone could, but after all, there's nothing likeable about extreme neurosis.

The Interpersonal's eyes widened.
"I stole that from you, m'dear," said the Oldest Member.

At any rate, and I will not go into all the other aspects of his neurotic problems, I have persevered in doing therapy because classical analysis is out of the question. Lately I've noticed that the subject of noodging is never far from my patient's lips, and now he seems to be correlating it with his obsession about the ERA.

He finally blurted out something about the "Noodge Factor."

"Do you mean that all the ERA women are noodges?"

"No, not at all," he said, although I knew that his wife—whom I had had the misfortune to interview—certainly fit into the category.

"Are you talking about women who noodge men about their health?" I asked after ten minutes of silence that shouldn't have bothered me—an experienced Freudian—quite so much.

He looked puzzled. He was sitting up, not lying down on the couch, because he was not an analytic patient. I am well aware that you non-Freudians sometimes do what you call depth analysis with the patient sitting up, but I firmly believe that the supine position on my comfortably battered couch (never re-cover your couch, colleagues. Show how used it has become.) is efficacious for . . . where was I?

"Puzzled," said one of the other Interpersonals.

Ah yes, after Mr. N seemed puzzled I explained, using reasoning taught me by a former patient. Most interesting.

"I suppose you have wondered," I began, "if a woman noodging a man about his health is perhaps trying to drive him prematurely senile in order to gain control . . ."

"What are you talking about?"

"Women who noodge. Women physicians are the worst . . ."

The Interpersonal squirmed.

"Oh," said Mr. N, "you're talking about the Be Careful Syndrome, that wearisome and endless repetition that drives anyone up the wall. The constant reiteration of 'Did you take your keys?' or 'Be careful crossing the street'—that sort of thing hammered into your ear as you're trying to leave the apartment."

"Yes, women can be impossible."

"Oh, my wife doesn't do that. She noodges about money and getting further up in the world, as if I weren't already too far up for my peace of mind."

"Then who?"

"My father. He's seventy-five and lives with us and noodges me to death. Always has."

"Then, the Noodge Factor . . ."

"Is an important, meaningful, and operational abstraction that I have discovered. Did you know that the word 'factor' has several definitions? In math it means one of two or more quantities having a designated product. I'm just not sure what the product is here."

There was another period of silence while Mr. N chewed his fingers and looked more depressed.

"So?"

He stared at the ceiling and twitched. "Perhaps it's related to the word 'factitious,' meaning 'contrived,' although I don't understand clearly whether or not there is a mystical import to that."

"And it's related to 'factious,' meaning 'divisive'?" I retorted, losing all Freudian control.

"Maybe you're right." He seemed to brighten up.

By this time I didn't have the faintest idea of what was going on and the hour—the one I had with him this morning —was nearly over. Then I remembered that my next patient had called to say that her car, in the suburbs, wouldn't start and she'd be late for her appointment because she'd have to take the train. I decided to be more flexible in my old age and to permit Mr. N to stay overtime. I would charge him only for an extra quarter of a session.

"Could you tell me the significance of all this?" I asked.

"Well, a factor may be a contrived product, but I prefer to think of it as something that actively contributes to an accomplishment, result, or process."

"Um?" I began to think that he had been memorizing the dictionary.

He ignored me and stared out my window across Central Park, where there had been a recent ERA march, and a woman's marathon was coming up soon. Now that the weather is warmer, it's fun to stroll in the park and watch the braless women go by, jiggling pleasantly and . . . where was I?

"Polishing your male chauvinism?" said the Interpersonal.

Not at all, although perhaps my patient was. At any rate, he did not seem to be enjoying the view, and time was passing.

"Perhaps you could tell me the connection between noodging and factors?"

"The Noodge Factor!" he exclaimed. "Don't you realize that there's a critical quantity of noodginess? I've been reading up on modern biological theories and although I don't understand them completely, it seems certain to me that life itself depends on a noodginess built into matter and energy —the interaction of atomic and subatomic particles; the testy pushing and shoving; the intrusive irritable encounters everywhere, at every rung of the ladder, fueling evolutionary progress . . ."

He went on like this at some length, mixing his metaphors and completely confusing me. At last he wound up his peroration.

". . . and don't you understand how crucial this is? How vital the Noodge Factor is? Without it, we're doomed!"

"But what is it?"

"I thought you were intelligent enough to see the point."

"Um," I said.

"I'll tell you. The Noodge Factor is the Critical Quantity Contributing to *Change!*"

"But . . ."

"And furthermore, since noodging itself is the driving force in evolution, equal rights will naturally be bad for the universe." He leaned forward, his voice dropping to a conspiratorial whisper.

"The damn ERA will destroy *Progress!*"

"Um?" I said, reflecting that people who work in important jobs on the national scene seem given to talking in capitalized words, and are especially fond of the word "progress," which they evidently equate with some sort of supernatural fulfillment that only they can decipher.

Mr. N hunched his shoulders, beetled his brows, and ground his teeth. "Surely you, a successful male like myself, must realize that Progress is necessary, and that it depends on Change, which depends on the Noodge Factor."

"Which depends on unequality of the sexes?" I said, trying to clear things up quickly because the doorbell had just rung, indicating that my tardy next patient had entered the waiting room.

"We of the superior sex should find that obvious," he said as he got up, his upper lip curled contemptuously.

He went out, leaving me feeling noodged to death. I am now curious about how my fellow Pshrinks would handle this problem.

As the Oldest Member finished speaking, the Interpersonal grinned and turned to the other females present.

"Hey, fellows," she said, "have you noticed how men get noodgier whenever we are at our most equal (and nowadays it may be illogical and ungrammatical but it's certainly pragmatic to refer to equality in terms of degrees), whenever women achieve equal status, power, or anything else that approaches equality, much less equal rights in terms of our still-born amendment?"

The other women nodded. One of the younger ones said, "And my father was—still is—exactly like Mr. N's."

"And my first analyst . . ."

"My boss at the hospital . . ."

"My *husband* . . ."

"And *my* husband . . ."

"There are entirely too many females in Pshrinks Anonymous," the Oldest Member suddenly announced. "I never noticed before how many have been creeping onto the roster."

"Perish forbid," said the Interpersonal. "Consider—it seems that your Mr. N really believes in the notion that if women get equal rights they will no longer have to noodge as much, and that will be bad for Progress. Poor Mr. N is concentrating too much on the Noodge *Factor,* forgetting that it is an abstraction that glosses over the essential fact and quantity of noodge itself. There is, after all, a good probability that there is a certain quantity of noodge present in the universe at any one time."

The Oldest Member glared at her. "Any second now I am going to start smoking my cigar."

"It's bad for you," said the Interpersonal. "Besides, I will explain. Tell your patient that if women ever get equal rights, they will have less cause to noodge, and men will have more cause, which solves everything."

"I don't get it."

"It's very simple. There is *Conservation of Noodge.*"

"Egad! Mr. N will love that argument, I hope, and perhaps get less preoccupied with the problem of equal rights once he grasps this theory—I gather that this *is* your theory—that there will always be enough noodging to keep the Noodge Factor operating to ensure Change."

"Exactly," said the Interpersonal. *"Male* noodging."

"Hear, hear!" said the other females.

"It is even possible—just barely, I admit—that the actual quantity of male chauvinism imbedded in those present—I name no names—will eventually diminish . . ."

The Oldest Member squelched the Interpersonal with a magnificent flourish of his cigar.

"No," he said, "I have changed my mind. You are wrong. The conservation principle will be upset. When women get equal rights and men get noodgier, we will still be doomed. Progress will grind to a halt. Evolutionary change will atrophy—and all due to the dangerous lack of parity that will inevitably occur."

"Why won't there be Conservation of Noodge?" asked the Interpersonal, somewhat plaintively.

"Ah," said the Oldest Member. "I'm glad you asked. It must be obvious to any thinking human that the proper amount of total noodge will not be conserved due to the dangerous persistence of female doctors—who will undoubtedly go on noodging helpless males about their health."

The chorus of male "ayes" outweighed the female groans.

THE ULTIMATE
BIOFEEDBACK DEVICE

Ensconced in a subbasement dining room where it would not infect the supposedly normal clientele of a small Manhattan hotel, the Psychoanalytic Alliance was well into its weekly luncheon of peculiar food and conversational strife.

"It won't do," said the Oldest Member, drumming his Freudian fingers on the table. His previous, more sulfurous remarks had excoriated the Adaptive Anchovies, then the Overcompensated Oxtail, and were now directed at certain Eclectic members of Pshrinks Anonymous who had rashly brought up the subject of various devices used in place of or in association with standard therapy.

"We are not here as mere therapists," said the Oldest Member loftily. "We are psychoanalysts tried and true, if of depressingly different faiths. I realize that in these decadent times we have had to let people into the club who are Not Classically Oriented (he glared at a female Interpersonal who had so far not said a word) but there have been ominous trends lately. Even some trained analysts are thinking about, talking about, writing about, and—heaven forfend—sometimes *using* machinery."

"I suppose you could call the couch a machine of sorts," ventured one Eclectic, "and our wristwatches . . ."

"I am talking about Machinery!" said the Oldest Member. "As I recall—and my memory is as good as ever—the luncheon conversation deteriorated when a few of you began discussing the latest research in biofeedback."

"Not a bizarre topic," said the Eclectic who had brought the subject up.

"Furthermore," said the Oldest Member, raising his voice, "as analysts *we* are *not* interested in biofeedback."

"Maybe Pshrinks should be," said the Interpersonal.

"Am I going to have trouble with you today?" asked the O.M., the villainous aspect of his bristling moustaches adulterated by their silver purity.

"Perish forbid," said the Interpersonal, staring at the cobwebs on the ceiling. Then she frowned.

"What is she frowning about?" asked a younger Freudian, one who had just finished an approved Continuing Medical Education course in biofeedback and was afraid to mention it.

"Ignore her," said the Oldest Member. "I happen to remember that she took some biofeedback courses once and was a dreadful bore for weeks."

"Maybe she's frowning about something meaningful," said a Jungian.

"Or far out," muttered an SF-addicted Pshrink.

"Nonsense," said the Oldest Member. "She's being seductive."

"Seductive?" said a Pshrink from the same institute as the Interpersonal. "To *us?*"

"She knows perfectly well that when a topic of conversation is raised and she contrives to look perturbed, we assume she is thinking about one of those bizarre cases of hers," said the O.M.

"I wonder," said the Interpersonal to the ceiling, "if we will continue to talk about robots in the third person—as if they were not present—when they become highly intelligent."

"Is this case about robots?" asked the Oldest Member.

"Not exactly, but there's a computer in it."

"And biofeedback?" asked the young Freudian eagerly.

The Oldest Member grabbed his moustaches by their waxed tips as if to ward off temptation. "No! Don't encourage her! Do we want to know *her* reason why Pshrinks should learn about biofeedback?"

No one replied verbally but there was considerable raising of eyebrows and slight forward inclination of heads.

The Oldest Member growled.

"Don't worry," said the Interpersonal, handing him her portion of Cyclothymic Chocolate, a pudding which combined light and dark chocolate in distinctly erotic patterns. "I don't have a case."

"Good," said the Oldest Member. "I confess that I like reading fiction about robots and computers but in reality they give me the willies."

"And well they might," said the Interpersonal. "To illustrate my point, I will now tell a true story."

The Oldest Member plunged into his dessert, recklessly devouring erotic patterns as he went.

When I was in one of the colleges I attended, [said the Interpersonal] I happened to share a suite with three roommates for about half the academic year. I will talk about one girl in particular—in my day, all roommates were unfortunately of the same sex as oneself—and I will refer to her as Bi, which is not her name.

Bi was younger than the rest of us because she had accelerated rapidly through school. Besides being a semigenius, she was also a girl who knew her own mind and used it to put down yours; and if that failed there was always the intimidation of her appearance, that of a female decathlon champ. I was moderately terrified of her and relieved when the dormitory was turned over to male veterans and we moved to separate houses. She transferred to another college the next year, so I lost track of her, not at all to my regret.

Many years later, to my astonishment, she surfaced in my

life as the wife of one of my husband's more remote professional acquaintances. She is a computer engineer; he is a
publisher. I had not yet met them, so I was curious when her
husband phoned and begged me to visit his wife, who would
not consult a psychiatrist but might talk things over with an
old friend.

Not wishing to argue over the definition of friends, I finally agreed to go to their suburban home, near her job in a
company which specializes in medical computers and sophisticated biofeedback devices.

Bi was alone, having sent her husband to the local bowling
club for the evening. From his photograph he definitely
resembled, even at his present age, a male decathlon
champ, so I assumed that it was either a marriage made in
heaven or the reason for the disguised consultation.

"It's not trouble with my husband," she announced, flex-
ing her muscles slightly in case I was inclined to disagree
with her. "It's my work. I was an electrical engineer and
now I'm a top computer designer. I've been working on an
experimental model that's part of our long-range program
for finding a cure for cancer by beefing up biofeedback so
patients will be able to monitor and destroy their own cancer cells."

"That's terrific!"

"Not yet," she said. "We'll get it eventually. I thought I
had but I haven't. Is there any point in talking to you? As I
distinctly remember, you were not good in physics."

"True."

"Weren't you the one who was giving the electricity lab
instructor ulcers until he made you promise never to throw
the master switch until he had checked the wiring of your
experiment?"

"Uh huh."

"How did you ever make Phi Bete? I looked you up before
I let my husband call you."

"Wouldn't it be easier if you just told me what the problem is?" I asked in approved Pshrink fashion, frequently a relief.

"Well, this experiment I've been running is having some very unusual results. I don't know whether to publish or see an extremely intelligent psychiatrist. I've compromised on you."

"Thanks. What's the experiment?"

"I've got an unusual computer interposed between two unusual devices. The first device senses the physioanatomical basis of human tissues, almost of single cells, perhaps of DNA molecules. I suppose you think that's impossible."

"I wouldn't know. What does the computer do?"

"Tunes into the readings as if the first device were an extension of its brain, and then goes into action, mentally speaking. It compares the readings of normal and abnormal DNA, of physiological processes, of all sorts of things which you have undoubtedly forgotten if you ever understood them in the first place; and then it sends integrated data and decisions to the second device, a complicated modification of an EEG machine plus an electrostimulator. The second device informs the patient in a nonverbal way that the lower levels of the mind can absorb and use without getting screwed up by the cerebral cortex, which is always lousing up attempts at getting the body to cure itself."

"I happen to think the cortex can do a good job at managing the body if used properly," I said. "After all, think of yogic control over smooth muscles—blood vessel dilation and contraction—and imagery techniques of mobilizing white blood corpuscles to eat up germs and cancer cells."

She sniffed scornfully. "*My* machine is aimed at pinpointing abnormalities and giving such accurate feedback that the patient will be able to correct things easily. I'm just having a little trouble with it at present, and the computer is so complex now that in order to find out what's wrong I think I'll have to take it apart, and that might destroy its abilities."

"Which are?"

She did not answer at once. She tapped her large white teeth and stared at me as if wondering whether or not I should be forced to get a security clearance. "I'm not sure. When I got the computer and the two devices complex enough to do what I expected them to do, I hooked myself into the system. I was feeling pretty good about the whole thing at the time, thinking that if Watson and Crick had had my machine to decipher DNA chemistry, they wouldn't have had to sweat so much getting to their Nobel Prize."

"A Nobel . . ."

"I expect one too, of course. The trouble was that I suddenly blacked out during the experiment and I think I had a dream."

"Ah," I said, feeling we had arrived at more secure ground. Dreams I know about.

"But on the other hand it probably wasn't a dream. All the images were overlapping and receding, on and on. I decided that whether or not I was dreaming, I was probably also getting some sort of reverberating feedback from the EEG apparatus."

"Electroencephalograms are readings of the electrical activity of the brain. They don't affect the brain."

"My machine is supposed to read out and also read in, giving feedback directly to the brain cells. Can't you grasp this simple point?"

"Not exactly, but persevere."

"I tried the machine several times on different days. Soon I began to be able to differentiate the images and concentrate on one to the exclusion of the others. The first one turned out to be somewhat amusing. I saw my grandmother."

"That's hardly an unusual dream image."

"I never actually saw that grandmother, who died when my mother was a kid. There aren't any photographs of her, and yet I saw her bodily configuration perfectly. She was naked and fairly young. I called my mother in Florida and asked if her mother had had inverted nipples."

"And she had," I said, since Bi seemed to have run down.

"Probably. Isn't it funny?"

"Is it?"

"I think you need a more impressive example," said Bi, who, I now remembered, had had large, everted nipples.

"When I concentrated again, I thought I saw my paternal grandmother, who's alive and within reach, but when I visited her I knew she wasn't the one. I asked her if *her* mother had a streak of bright gold in her brown pubic hair when she was young. After exploding, Grandmother admitted that her older brother might know and even tell, since he was without shame, like her granddaughter. I wrote to him, Grandmother translated his answer, and threw it in the fire."

"Your computer must be reading different parts of your DNA that you got from different ancestors," I said.

"I'm certain of it. Then the EEG feedback is being analyzed, reconstructed, and augmented by the computer so that I end up seeing images of the entire ancestor. I presume that I don't have to explain to a doctor why I can see paternal ancestors as well as maternal, since my DNA comes from both sperm and ova. My husband understood that finally. What he doesn't understand is why I'm spending so much time with my computer. It's possible he's a trifle upset over the fact that I've fallen in love with one of my own ancestors."

"What!"

"I thought psychoanalysts aren't supposed to look surprised."

"I'm here as an ex-roommate, remember? Which ancestor have you fallen for? It was basketball players when I knew you."

"Well, I pushed the images back and forth, and then back and back, or the computer did—I'm not sure anymore who's doing what—and bits of DNA from all sorts of people are in my cells. Most of them are ugly and uninteresting, but one I recognized. He's not exactly handsome, but incredibly intriguing and mysteriously sexy, the sort I wouldn't have considered when I was young."

"Who?"

She smiled coyly, which caused her to resemble *Tyrannosaurus rex* pretending to be friendly while closing in. "One of my great-grandfathers was supposed to be upper-class English, according to family legend. Now I'm certain that he was descended from a good family indeed, in a bastard line, which makes me related to a lot of people, including Darwin's Captain Fitzroy . . ."

"Are you trying to tell me that you think you are descended from one of the illegitimate offspring of Charles II?"

"When the computer and I focused properly, that's who I saw. At first I couldn't believe it was really Charles II, but the likeness to the portraits is unmistakable. And don't go telling me it's wish fulfillment or pretensions to royalty, or a secret girlhood crush on Charles II, because I was never good at history and while I enjoyed the British TV production about the monarchy, I never had any special interest in Charles. The family legend never went that far back. But I did, and let me tell you, he's a magnificent specimen of malehood when seen nude."

"I'm sure Nellie and the others thought so," I said, observing the increasingly hectic color of her cheeks and the stubborn set to her chin. "Is this all that's bothering you?"

"You don't believe me."

"I'll believe almost anything about computers and biofeedback, so please tell me if there's anything else."

She got up and strode around the living room, kicking moodily at articles of furniture. Automatically, I tensed my leg muscles, ready to spring aside if necessary.

She was silent for so long that I got impatient. Glancing at my watch, I tried to hurry things, which is never productive unless a Pshrink knows what she's doing, which I didn't. "For hell's sake, Bi, have you been imagining things? I assume that all your ancestors you tune into via your DNA are going to be youngish because the computer would reconstruct them as they looked at the time their DNA was passed on, or before—not later. Are you spending your time with this computer imagining that Charles II is having sex—"

"I tried," she said absently. "I tried hard to get inside his head and sense what was or had been going on with his body, but all I got was pictures of the interior decor of a castle. Maybe I was looking through his eyes or maybe I was imagining. I don't know. Then I thought that I'd try further back than Charles, but it was terribly confusing because there are so many roots. Finally I got a clear image of someone's arm. Mine. Big, covered with red hair, and full of itchy bugs. It scared the hell out of me."

"The bugs?"

"No. The fact that this time I was inside the person. I *was* that person, a man; and after believing that I understood men, I realized I didn't understand *him* at all, what he was thinking or talking."

"What language?"

"How would I know? He had a brand on the back of his hand that I couldn't decipher. Like this." She drew it for me.

"Looks like a rune."

"A ruin? He may have been lousy, but he was no ruin."

"Rune as in Norse. We can postulate that if you are genuinely related to the English kings your ancestry goes back to the Normans and thus to their Viking ancestors."

She brightened up at once, and I didn't have the heart to tell her that I'd omitted the fact that the Vikings inserted their DNA into a good many—er—countries.

"You've done some good after all," said Bi magnanimously. "There's no reason for me to have trepidations about following out my ancestry. I might be able to experience being prehuman, or even trace out my evolution through the animal kingdom. You aren't one of those simplistic creationists who doesn't believe in evolution, are you?"

"Of course not," I said, reflecting that while Bi was a genius of sorts in engineering, she had been and apparently still was naive about many other things. "Don't be surprised if you get blurrier images farther back than *Homo sapiens*. Remember that many of the DNA molecules in any person living now have been replenished by atoms from food sources, so that what you inherited from very far back is bound to be weak as far as the computer is concerned."

"I suppose you're right," she said, obviously bored. "I think it's time I called my husband home from bowling. He'll get used to my admiration for Charles II. He won't let me hook him up to the computer because he says he read somewhere that no man is free who has a thousand ancestors."

"I think your husband is smarter than we are."

"We?"

"I'd love to try the machine."

"I'll think about it," said Bi with the finality which says one hasn't got a prayer. I suddenly remembered that she had always been fussy about her possessions being used by anyone else, and I was annoyed. I happen to be a full quarter English, so if anyone is likely to be descended from Charles II . . . but I digress.

"You certainly do," said the Oldest Member, who was irrationally certain that somewhere in the past he and Freud had a common ancestor.

About a month later [continued the Interpersonal], I got a call from a psychiatrist who said he was in charge of Bi's case at her local hospital. It seemed that she had been overcome by anxiety while using her computer, and was under sedation.

"You sound as if she's also in a straitjacket," I said.

"Not yet," said the psychiatrist. "Please tell me everything she told you about her work with the computer. She hasn't told anybody much about it, not even her husband."

"Do you have a signed release?" I asked, remembering more about my ex-roommate, who had been given to threats of lawsuit over trifles, like the time the school paper misprinted her I.Q.

"No."

"I think I'd rather see her," I said.

So I did. They had withheld sedatives; and she was out of bed, sitting up in a chair in her private room. Her face seemed to be carved out of white plaster that might crumble at any moment, and she wouldn't talk.

I talked. She wouldn't respond.

I got up and walked around, kicking the furniture. Finally I said, "Okay, you're the brightest student in school; but you're dumb in the school of life, which is what I've been studying for years. I also know more about people and what happens to them when they decide to collapse. Has your failure with your computer—not finding a cure for cancer—made you decide to enjoy being a mess? When all the other roommates you used to intimidate hear about this . . ."

"You wouldn't!"

"Actually, I don't threaten patients; but you're only an ex-roommate, and you've got plenty of ego left, and I'm not in the mood to let *you* intimidate me with this behavior."

"I never could stand you," she said slowly, "but you're not as dumb as I used to think. You believed me about Charles, didn't you?"

"I believe that you and that computer of yours may possibly have tuned into DNA molecules that go way back. If you want to drive yourself crazy with a mad passion over a rapscallion of an ancestor . . ."

"He's gorgeous—but he's not the problem. I should have stayed with him."

"I don't understand."

"I should have stayed on that level. You were right about the DNA readout getting hazier and hazier the farther back I went. But I went back, and back, and back . . ." Her voice died out and she began to shake.

"Well, what happened? Scared by *Homo erectus?* Therapsid reptiles? Slimy amphibians? Bony fishes? Amphioxus? Coelenterates?" I paused and she stared at me. "*Amoebae?*"

"Hell no. I left DNA behind."

"What do you mean?"

"You're the biologist," she said scornfully. "You know that DNA is composed of nucleotides. I looked it up."

"All life is organic chemistry if you dig deep enough."

"That's just it. I had the feeling that I'd latched onto a single atom. There were many I experimented with, but they all petered out, so I assume they came from outside my direct line of animal ancestors. I started looking for atoms that have been with my DNA from the beginnings of life on Earth."

"That would be marvelous!"

"Not so marvelous. I think I did it, but I didn't enjoy the trip. Maybe it was a carbon atom, but then it wasn't. I pushed back and back and it seemed as if I were part of a sea—"

"Oh, that's easy," I interrupted, trying to show off my biology. "You were still in a primitive organic molecule in the primordial soup that the sea turned into on Earth, according to one theory I like."

"A sea of *light*, stupid! I may have been in the other kind of sea earlier; but by the time I pushed hard enough, I was in light, and then back into something terrible; and I wasn't even an atom. I was smaller, and trapped in a furnace. I tried to get out by going back even farther, and that was the worst of all. I lost myself. My individuality. I had no identity; and if there's one thing I have always had, it's a definite identity! That's when I broke loose from the computer and cracked up."

The white plaster was beginning to crumble, so I hurriedly said, with more than a little exaggeration, since I was still thinking hard, "I can explain it all. With your permission, I'll talk to your doctor and sign you out and we'll go to your lab. Try the computer again and then hook me into the same setting that upset you."

"You'd do that for me, when we never liked each other?"

I had to be honest about that. "Mostly for myself."

I was now reminded that her laugh had always resembled the braying of a mule, but it was a relief to hear it.

We went back to her lab; and after she found the setting, she got out of the chair, trembling again. "I suppose I trust you, even if you did nearly drive me bananas when you'd stuff each day's newspaper under your mattress when you had the bunk above me."

"I had to. The springs sagged."

"You had no regard for my feelings, which are terribly sensitive. I hated waking up and seeing old headlines above me. And I really hate having you commune with my computer."

"That's obvious," I said, sitting down in the chair. She hooked me up, breathing heavily as she did it; and after a while I said, "Show me how to fiddle with the settings to bring myself up to a more advanced level of evolution."

She did; and I did; and after a bit of surreptitious trembling myself, I said, "I think I've found your problem. Would you get me a glass of water?"

While she was gone, I fiddled with the setting again, letting her catch me at it as she returned with the glass. "Try it at the setting I've got now," I said.

After a while she said, "I think this is the same thing I showed you before, and I hate it. You put the setting back where it had originally been, didn't you?"

"Yes," I lied.

"Then what have we got? What unpleasant state did I get to? That terrible sensation of having no identity, and then when I go forward in time, I'm terribly small and moving awfully fast . . ."

"Whoa!" I said, as her voice rose to a screech. "Remember that when I used the computer I experienced my own preorganic evolution from tuning into whatever molecules have been with me and my ancestors all along. I did the same thing you did. Now two of us have had this charming adventure, and you aren't alone. None of us has ever been alone, come to think of it. Life on Earth developed all of a piece, all interrelated."

"Very poetic. That doesn't explain anything."

"It does. I strongly recommend that you don't make the computer push you back as far as you did, because it will always feel awful. Would anyone like to experience, for any length of time, what happens in a supernova?"

"You're kidding."

"No. Biological evolution is an outgrowth of the evolution of organic molecules, and you can't have organic molecules without atoms like carbon, oxygen, and nitrogen, which are made in the furnace of a star."

"Our sun? Is that where I was?"

"No. That's not where *our* carbon, nitrogen, and oxygen came from. In our volume of space, there were, previously, massive stars which manufactured heavier atoms in their private nuclear furnaces; and when one eventually exploded in a supernova, a cloud of gas containing all those elements spewed out. The force of expansion drove this contaminated gas into other gas clouds and when our second-generation sun coalesced out, it was accompanied by the coalescing planets of its solar system, rich in those elements made by the earlier star."

"The supernova would be that hideous sensation of moving out very fast in a sea of light, but earlier—when I lost myself—"

"You pushed back to when the earlier star was young and you were only a proton in some helium or hydrogen atom. It's understandable that the image—or sensation, or whatever the computer synthesized—was so vivid. Maybe only a portion of your DNA came from that Viking, for instance, but *all* of Earth except its hydrogen and helium goes back to atoms formed by nuclear fusion in primary stars which exploded."

Bi shuddered. "I won't go back there again. Never. I don't like being only a proton." She stretched and yawned, always a good sign after someone has been anxious and intense. "Astronomy bores me anyhow. I like history now that I'm middle-aged."

"And what did Charles II look like without his wig?" I asked.

The Interpersonal stopped speaking and reached for an after-dinner mint.

"Are we supposed to gather that your friend is now out of the hospital permanently?" asked the Oldest Member.

"I hope so."

"I don't believe a word of any of this," said a studiously skeptical Pshrink.

"It's quite true," said the Interpersonal. "There really is a computer like that and heaven help us if it ever gets into the hands of the public."

"On the contrary, it's heaven-sent," said a new Pshrink who was having trouble building up his practice. "When people start going back into their ancestry think of all the resulting psychopathology!"

"Wait till the creationists hear about it," said the Oldest Member happily. "They'll have apoplexy and become extinct, one hopes."

The latest Youngest Member, the token psychiatric resident-in-training, cleared his throat nervously and said, "How can your story be true when you said you lied to Bi?"

"Astute of you to notice," said the Interpersonal. "I had to lie. I was afraid Bi would not be able to stand the truth—that I had switched the setting."

"I don't get it," said the Oldest Member.

"When I hooked into the machine," said the Interpersonal, "I sensed what had frightened Bi. I switched it forward in time and found another event which I thought I could more easily explain to her. Then I pretended to let her catch me switching it back again, so that what she saw the second time was not what had scared her."

"I am thoroughly confused, and I knew it was a mistake to let you talk," said the Oldest Member. "You told Bi that she'd seen a primary, first-generation star which exploded into a supernova. Didn't she?"

"Yes, the second time. What she found first, when she went back far enough—what she showed me when I tried the computer the first time—was the early history of that first star, which coalesced out of another sea of brightness."

"The Big Bang!" said the Youngest Member.

"That's right. The very beginning of the universe. It's logical, isn't it, that if you push back far enough in time, you'll get to the original explosion that started everything, that everything—every part of every one of us—comes from."

"Why didn't it drive you crazy too?" asked an Eclectic.

"Because I suspected that's what she'd found. It would be an awful shock to anyone just looking for biological ancestors. She got so far back that she did lose all identity, even that as a quark in the hypothetical quark soup that the universe may have been before the Big Bang. Poor Bi. She's one of those people for whom things have to be individual and relevant and personally important. For her, nothingness is terrifying."

"Nothingness?"

"How else would you describe the sea of nothing-like-anything? The sea without boundaries, without form and dimension, a void with only potential—"

"Couldn't you be a little less biblical?" asked the Oldest Member.

"Having been there, I assure you there's nothing biblical about it. It's not even scary if you consider that absolute nothingness is at the same time everything. At least it felt as if everything were everything. As if it were Home. I was pleased that I haven't been studying Taoism and Zen for nothing—or do I mean that I *have* been studying them for Nothing?"

"I can't stand this," said the Oldest Member. "I'm going home, and I don't mean to some primordial condition of the universe."

"I think you and your ex-roommate have merely been playing with a computer that whomps up fantasies for you," said a Pshrink who specialized in taking his patients on guided trips through the unconscious. "You see what you want to see, the way patients interpret their dreams."

"And the way some Pshrinks tend to interpret their patients' dreams?" said the Interpersonal.

"I suppose, m'dear," said the Oldest Member, who somehow never left when he threatened to, "that you ought to admit it was only a fantasy. It would be better for your mental health."

"Perhaps you'll all have a chance at the machine someday," said the Interpersonal. "You'd better, because you ought to know what's going to happen to other people who try it. You'll have to teach people what is already being taught in simpler forms of biofeedback—that a person can *choose* what he does with it. You can choose to raise blood pressure instead of lowering it, for instance; but if you're interested in curing your hypertension, you won't. You can also choose what reading to get from Bi's machine—the state of health of a cell's DNA, or where it's been."

The O.M. smoothed down his moustache. "You almost persuade me. Nevertheless, I refuse to approve of your flights—perhaps of fancy—into the past with that infernal machine. I do not approve of computers with preoedipal fixations, uncontrollable ids, and delusions of omnipotence."

"Um, yes," said the Interpersonal. "As a matter of fact, the last time I talked to Bi, I asked her about the possibility of constructing a new machine with safeguards built in to make it focus only on the abnormal DNA of an actual or potential cancer. Perhaps the new machine will ultimately enable humans to cure their own cancers. In the meantime, the original machine can be used exclusively and cautiously for research that I hope to hear about—"

"But *not* participate in!" said the Oldest Member severely. "We may have ideational conflicts, but I prefer that you retain *your* identity."

"Thank you! I shall endeavor to retain my own peculiarities uncontaminated by exposure to ancestral personalities or cosmic togetherness."

"Harrumph! I did not mean that improvement was unnecessary. For instance, I am appalled that you seem unconcerned about your ex-roommate's psychodynamics, which are clearly in need of intensive analysis."

"On the contrary," said the Interpersonal. "I have forcefully recommended psychoanalysis for Bi's neurotic preoccupations. Charles II, forsooth!"

THE CURIOUS
CONSULTATION

"I don't see why we have to be Pshrinks *Anonymous,*" said one of the members of the Psychoanalytic Alliance luncheon club. "This pretending that we don't know who we are . . ."

"Ah," said one of the Interpersonals.

The Oldest Member (who relished his title, stolen from Wodehouse) looked at her suspiciously. "There's no point in discussing the use of our anonymity. It's a great relief not having to remember names."

"What's in a name?" said the Youngest Member.

"You'd better not say that," said the Interpersonal.

"I would ask why not," said the Oldest Member, "but I realize that posing such a question might make this entrée even more inedible than it looks. Whose turn was it to plan the menu?"

"Mine," said a Behaviorist who was also, unaccountably, a graduate Pshrink. "This is a new dish—Conditioned Capon."

The Oldest Member squinted at his plate. "Full of frustrated sexuality, no doubt." He picked up a particularly phallic drumstick and turned to the Interpersonal. "I suppose you have an atrocious case history to report?"

"Indubitably," she said.

"What's in a name?" may well be the question of the year, or of the century, for all I know [said the Interpersonal]. Before I explain that, I must go back to the days when I was still in analytic school, in my late twenties. Some of my classmates were much older, having spent years as psychotherapists before deciding to get analytic training. One of these was a man about forty who already had a thriving psychiatric practice and would occasionally send me referrals, usually female patients whose transferences to him had gone out of control. Not that he was astoundingly attractive, being medium tall, medium fat, and medium homely. Perhaps it was his medium motherliness that got to them.

I shall refer to this classmate as Dr. S, or Stuffy as we always called him.

When I first knew Stuffy, he was having trouble getting through analytic training because he seemed to have no analytic intuition and tended to stay stuck in the role of a benevolently supportive doctor, unable to master the nuances of Pshrinkhood. The rest of us in the class thought of him as a prosaically unflappable nonentity with no imagination.

I was therefore surprised one day when he called me to ask if I would do a special one-shot consultation on a male patient of his. Old Stuffy sounded almost agitated.

"I can't understand what's happened," he said. "The treatment seemed to be going well, even a little analytically, although it wasn't one of the cases I'm presenting to my supervisors. The patient seems to be running into—well, er —severe neurotic difficulties. I thought maybe you would figure out what's going on."

"Why don't you send the patient to one of the older analysts at the Institute? One of your supervisors?"

"And have everyone know I'm a failure at doing analysis?"

Stuffy always seemed to devote himself to being the kind of conventional success that does not attract attention. He seemed addicted to suits and ties and ideas that were drab and ordinary. His hair was short, his voice bland; he ate steak and potatoes; his office was decorated in motel modern. His wife had divorced him two years previously, presumably on grounds of terminal boredom.

"Well," I said, "why me?"

"I understand that you read that sci-fi stuff."

"SF! And what's that got to do with your patient?"

I could hear Stuffy's gulp galloping across Ma Bell's wires. "I've taken it up with my analyst, but she's no help. She doesn't read science fiction and you do. You must see this patient."

"Aren't you going to tell me anything about what you hope to learn from the consultation?"

"No. I might prejudice you. I'll merely tell you that the patient is a twenty-two-year-old white male physicist with a Ph.D. and a good research job. I've been treating him for a year. He had a certain amount of performance anxiety at work and in his social life, but it's been clearing up nicely, and I was thinking we could terminate therapy soon."

"He seems to be getting worse for an unknown reason?"

"Oh, the reason isn't unknown. I just don't understand it. I want to know your opinion."

"Filtered through my knowledge of science fiction," I said sarcastically.

"Exactly. Please help!"

When we hung up, my previous mental image of Dr. S was shaken. Was this the Stuffy I knew, who had apparently been born middle-aged and complacent? When his wife left, he hadn't given any evidence of being rattled; and none of his supervisors in analytic school had ever been able to ripple his surface. This patient had, for that word "help" ended in a plaintive squeak.

Suddenly I reheard Stuffy's description of the patient who was to call me for an appointment. Had I heard correctly? A working physicist, complete with Ph.D., who was only twenty-two years old?

The patient came for a consultation at the end of that week. I will call him Nemo, although of course that was not his name. He was tall, thin, and as knobby as if he'd been constructed out of elbows; and his bristly red hair stuck out at the temples almost at right angles. He appeared to be so adolescent that I prepared myself for a consultation centered on his delayed emotional maturation.

"I'm supposed to be a genius . . . ," he announced, stumbling over the rug and falling sideways into the patient's chair. Rubbing the bony knee he had presumably just bruised, he added, ". . . in science. Mentally. I haven't been expert at the rest of life but I'm learning, or I will if you shrinks can keep me out of Bellevue Psycho." He reached up with both hands and tugged at the juts of red hair as if to strengthen what lay between them.

"Who thinks you ought to go there?" I asked, wondering if he were as anxious as he looked.

"I do. Maybe Stuffy does."

"How do you know his nickname?"

"One of my older cousins went to medical school with him. Said Stuffy was reasonably intelligent, sympathetic, and knowledgeable about how to get along in the ordinary world, so I went to him for psychotherapy. I like Stuffy."

He frowned at me. "I know I've upset him, but I can't say I approve of this consultation business. You're too young. I don't like talking to a shrink who is my own age."

Although I was then still on his side of thirty, I tried to nod analytically while arranging my face into what I hoped was an aspect both mature and sophisticated. I said, "You don't have to talk to me, but as long as you're here you might try it, especially since I'm actually a lot older than you are."

"Oh. Really?" He bent forward to study me. "Yeah. You are."

I found one of my hands hovering upward to grasp my own hair at the temples. As I fought to control this phenomenon, I said, "Then suppose we talk about why you and Stuffy think you need Bellevue."

"Because of a dream. I had it a few weeks ago, after a frustrating day of playing chess with the lab computer, which I can't make smart enough to beat me. Nothing's been the same since. It was pleasant in the dream at first—I was floating in a warm and sort of homey dark. Undoubtedly my first authentic back-to-the-womb experience. Stuffy loved it."

I recalled that in analytic school Stuffy's supervisors were complaining about his penchant for clinging to the safe rigidities of antiquated Freudian concepts which seem to explain everything . . .

"Antiquated!" roared the Oldest Member, whose thinking had congealed half a century previously. "Nonsense!"

. . . I decided [continued the Interpersonal, patting the Oldest Member's elegantly jacketed arm] that I had better not comment.

"All at once," said Nemo, "I heard a word."

There was a long pause, during which he squirmed in the chair.

"What was it?"

He took a deep breath, expelled it forcefully, cleared his throat, and said something—a word, if it was that, so long and complicated that it sounded like several utterly weird syllables welded together to create a more bizarre piece of language than I had ever heard.

"Damn," said Nemo. "I did it badly again. That's approximately, but not quite, what I heard in the dream, in the warm dark; and I can't get it out of my head. I think about it all the time. It's driving me crazy not to be able to reproduce it completely accurately, for myself or for anyone else to hear. That and the implications. Did you by chance get any —um—sensation when I said it?"

"No."

"Stuffy seemed to, but I reproduced it better for him."

"Do you, or did you get a sensation?" I asked.

He was silent, and didn't squirm at all. I was disquieted by his physical stillness and blank face, as if he were listening intently. I was also annoyed at Stuffy for referring what seemed to be an acutely hallucinating patient, without warning me first.

After what seemed like hours of silence, I said, "Are you still with me?"

Immediately, his facial muscles formed themselves into another expression of acute anxiety. "You would have to talk, wouldn't you! I thought I'd memorize it that time."

"You were *hearing* it?"

"*Remembering* it. I'm not hallucinating! It's probably not important at all. I don't know why it bugs me this way except that I think . . ."

I waited, and then said, "Think what?"

Nemo laughed. I had the distinct impression that he was changing the subject. He shrugged and said, "Forget it. The noise I thought I heard in my dream is probably just a swear word my unconscious invented to use against that stupid computer. Or maybe it's what Stuffy tried to convince me it was, a memory of an unpleasant noise my mother made when I was *in utero*. Wouldn't it be funny if the fate of the world was decided because of an unusual maternal sneeze, burp, or fart?"

"Fate of the world?"

Nemo paled. "I didn't realize I said that. Damn."

"Explain."

"You remind me of my computer when you do that. I've programmed it to show a big question mark on the tape when it doesn't understand the instruction, which is most of the time. It's incredibly stupid. Someday computers will be smarter, and won't fill a room the way the one at our lab does."

"You might still try explaining . . ."

"I don't want to. Forget the whole thing. It was just a silly noise in a dream. Something I ate, no doubt."

I had now run into a dead end in my investigation of what we Pshrinks call the chief complaint. It was time to investigate the history of the patient. Fortunately I had already learned to schedule extra time for consultations so that the patient would not have to leap out of the room at fifty minutes.

"You mentioned your mother. Perhaps you could tell me something about her," I began, imitating one of my more obsessional supervisors' history-taking routine.

I heard about his mother, who didn't sound much better or worse than any who have had to cope with children equipped with unexpectedly high I.Q.s. Ditto his father, his ordinary siblings, the family dog and parakeet, the near and far relatives, the important teachers and camp counselors, chums and girlfriends, and so on. Since Nemo was an experienced patient, he rattled through all this in a remarkably short time.

It seemed that aside from his certifiable case of genius, Nemo had no obvious history that could definitely account for the development of his current problem. He didn't take drugs or alcohol, did not suffer social or sensory deprivation, had no unusual sexual difficulties, enjoyed his friends and family and particularly his career. I did not believe that he was being made ill by his interest in science fiction, or his career in the new and burgeoning field of developing artificial intelligence . . .

"That only goes to prove that your own neurotic bias got in the way of thinking clearly and analytically about this patient," said the Oldest Member severely.

. . . and [continued the Interpersonal after a slight groan] it seemed to me that up to the moment Nemo had

that mysterious dream, he'd been an example of the research evidence that people with high intelligence—even
those addicted to science fiction—are more often happy and
successful than not.

"We're back to the noise in your head," I finally said,
deliberately choosing "noise" instead of "word" so that he
would want to answer. He did.

"I tell you it's not a noise—it's a word! In fact, it feels as if
it's a *name*, a name stuck in my memory that I can't
reproduce and somehow I must."

"Why?"

"I don't know."

"What did you think was making the noise. I mean, saying
the name."

"What's the use of telling you, since you'll only say that it
came out of my brain, so that the only person saying the
name is me."

"We can always return to that hypothesis. What do you
imagine—no, let me ask it another way. In the dream itself,
what seemed to be saying the name?"

"That's just it. *I* was. Or I was tuning into something I was
hearing and I was naming it—oh hell, I don't know." He put
his head in his hands. "I'm falling apart. Ever since this
happened I've been studying and studying. Did you know
that names have mystical meaning and frightening power in
most mythologies? Did you know how the ancient Hebrews
never said or wrote the name of their god but instead used a
word meaning 'That Which Is'? That in the biblical tales
Adam was supposed to have power over each thing he
named? That in many cultures children are named after
animals in order to incorporate the desired traits of the
animal, that names are part of many taboo practices, many
rituals of adolescence in which a new name is given, many
rites of kingship in which a new title is bestowed by grace of
the deity—"

"But—"

"And get this. The word *nāma* in Buddhism really means all mental processes collectively speaking—"

"You do not appear to be telling me what you thought, in the dream, was making the noise."

He paid no attention. "I can remember the sound, but I can't see it. I'm not a very visual person anyway—much more aural—yet I ought to be able to visualize how the word might be spelled in English letters, but I can't. I've studied up on phonetics and dipped into linguistics, but so far it hasn't helped, and religion is even more useless, although of course I've wondered about that. As I told you, I'm a scientific agnostic from a nonreligious family and I just won't believe that this is my unconscious telling me I ought to get religion!"

"What made the noise?" I repeated. When patients ostentatiously avoid answering a question, it usually means something; or so my supervisors were telling me.

"And did you know that *nama*, without the line over the first *a*, is also the word for 'name' in Old English? Fascinating. There's a famous one-syllable word used as a mantra, or part of a mantra, in many oriental religions. *Om* is supposed to be the syllable of the supreme reality, or—if you want to get deistic and into the thinking of the common herd—oriental this time, the name for the trinity of the gods."

"Did you tell Stuffy what, in your opinion, made the noise?"

Nemo scowled. "That's a silly question. Stuffy's upset enough after hearing the almost-good-enough reproduction of the noise I made in his office once."

"All right. Protect him. I'm only the consultant. What made—no." I stopped, studied the agitation in his face, and decided to take a calculated risk. *"Who* made the noise?"

"Very smart," said Nemo bitterly. "Now I'm supposed to go out on a limb with speculation, after which you will demolish me by saying that I was tuning into a memory of a name from the past, some garbled version a child would invent, and I can't recapture it because I had lots of ambivalent feelings about whatever or whomever from the past."

"Well, I—"

"You needn't be such an ass! You should have figured out already that what scares me out of my pants is the possibility that the noise, word, name, or whatever was never heard on Earth before!"

Nemo flung himself out of the chair and paced across my small office, hitting his head with his fist. I was beginning to get scared. Perhaps he was more psychotic than I realized and I was making him worse.

"Maybe," I said tentatively, "you'd better go back to telling me what you thought the word meant, or what the name applies to."

He stopped in front of the window, which had a view of Central Park. "Look out there at the world. Reality. Trees and grass and stones—and people—maybe I don't like people much, although I do get along better, and my fiancée thinks I'm getting terrific in bed, and I've got all these ideas for research into computer technology . . ."

I waited. He babbled on and then sat down again, staring into the middle distance. He looked as if he were listening, and not to me.

He sighed. "I can't figure out the dream. And I am going crazy. I suppose it's off to Bellevue Psycho."

"Don't be silly," I snapped countertransferentially. "You'll have a worse time figuring out the dream if you're inside a hospital."

His eyes widened. "Do you think I'm acting crazier and crazier to impress Stuffy and you with how helpless I feel? To make you put me away so I won't have to do anything but work on the mantra?"

"Admirably reasoned. Are you now saying that the noise was a mantra?"

"No. I don't know. I might as well tell you the rest of what I've been thinking. Then you'll really send me to Bellevue."

"Sending people to Bellevue against their will isn't usually done unless they are suicidal or homicidal; and even if you were both, I might have a little trouble taking you there, since you're bigger than I am. What's the truth?"

He seemed to relax, now that I had declared my human frailty. "I'll try to tell you, if I can. You see, I'm scared by the noise I heard, and I don't know if it's the implications of what the word or name could mean, or of what could be saying the word, or of what I'm like if it's just coming out of me. Sitting here with you I've realized that poor Stuffy couldn't help me answer those questions, and you can't. Nobody can. I have to decide for myself."

"Or you could just forget it and go about daily life."

"But you don't understand! If I forget, somebody else may happen on it and do something great with it. Win the Nobel Prize or something. I have to confess that I have a yen to win the Nobel Prize, but so do all my colleagues."

"So?"

"You're right. Now let me try to get into my reasoning, simplified for your intelligence." Nemo leaned toward me again, lecturing as if he were an elderly professor. "Let's begin with the idea that if the noise is just a noise, then it takes intelligence—in this case, human intelligence—to turn the noise into a name."

"I'm following you so far," I said rather bitterly.

"Good. Now if the act of naming is an act that confers or evokes power, then if anybody duplicates the noise correctly or names whatever it is we're naming, then *Something Will Happen!*"

As I have recounted previously, I have had vast experience with people who speak in capitalized words, to say nothing of italics; and I strongly suspected that Nemo was thinking in both.

"Oh well," I said, yawning slightly to indicate that he'd have to do better than that to get me anxious, "I suppose you have a few fantasies about that."

Nemo grabbed his hair with his hands. "Now don't imagine that I believe anything as downright crazy as the idea that by pronouncing the name I'll turn into a god, because that's not how it felt. In the dream, when I tuned in to the noise and said it back as if it were a name, I knew that suddenly there was something listening. Worst of all, I had the feeling that I had *caused* it to be able to listen!"

"What do you have in mind about that?" I asked in the approved analytic response.

Nemo bit his lip. "Suppose the word is actually a call signal for an intelligent alien race?"

"That's a rather hackneyed SF plot, but I suppose that wouldn't mean anything to your unconscious."

"Very funny. Explain away my awful memory of feeling that whatever was listening was very, very big."

I yawned again.

Nemo ground his teeth and seemed about to burst forth in anger at me when he looked stunned. "I was so angry with you that it must have jarred loose my memory, because I've remembered something else from the dream. There was the awful suspicion that the listener—that gigantic entity—was also myself. Is this just galloping grandiosity?"

"Possibly. You seem like a good candidate for it. But perhaps your giant brain can think of something in addition to that."

Nemo shook his head despairingly and leaned back, staring off into space to my right, where there happens to be a bookcase.

"I see you have some books on Zen," he said.

"Yes. Does that bring anything to mind?"

"I'm into Zen myself. I suppose you're hinting that I am part of the Universe, and maybe it is rather grandiose of me to think of myself as naming the totality, conferring a title upon it as it comes alive . . . wow! Am I psychotic enough to believe that I'm making the Universe come alive by giving it a name? A perfect name?"

"It sounded to me as if you meant, earlier, that the noise you heard had always been there and you tuned in."

"That's right. But you're the psychiatrist! Aren't you going to insist that I made the whole thing up? After all, the dream is my invention, isn't it?"

"Yes, but I can't help remembering that scientists often have strange dreams that incorporate aspects of their thinking about reality, aspects they haven't become conscious of yet. Remember Kekule deciphering the structure of the benzene ring after dreaming about a snake that grabbed its own tail?"

"Okay, okay. I'm a genius, but I'm still scared. My imagination is going wild. How do we know what the Universe is going to be like when it's a live, conscious entity?"

"Damned if I know. Aren't you really worrying about your own sense of magical power?"

He laughed. "The funny thing is that other people think geniuses have magical power, but they don't. What I felt in the dream was magical maybe only in the sense of being beyond ordinary science. That's what I've always wanted, to be the sort of scientist who goes far beyond the science of his own day. Is that what all this boils down to, simple wish fulfillment?"

"That would be convenient," I said. "Have you told me everything about the dream?"

The smile died on his face. "Hell. You've made me remember one more thing. It was—hell, I won't believe that. It's not important."

"Your time is almost up. Maybe for completeness' sake you'd better say—"

"Oh hell, all right. It doesn't fit anyway with our beautiful theory of intelligence as part of the Universe coming alive. I like that, and I think I can find a use for it. Maybe eventually I'll be able to reproduce the sound perfectly and pass it on for others to play with. In the meantime, Stuffy will just have to keep himself from going 'round the bend—"

"What!"

"I forgot to tell you. I think I injured Stuffy in some way when I reproduced the sound almost perfectly for him. I don't know why. But I have faith in him. He's sane and not too dumb and he'll be all right."

I was beginning to grind my own teeth. "What were you going to say that you remembered?"

"Oh, it was nothing. By the way, did you ever read Clarke's 'The Nine Billion Names of God'?"

"Yes, but . . ."

"Great story, but that's not how things are going to be. The Universe won't end if that name I heard is duplicated correctly, because to paraphrase the old joke, there isn't any God and He's not going to notice. Nevertheless, when intelligence has a readily usable way of tuning into ultimate reality, when the name begins to *Work*, then watch out, Universe!"

"You still haven't told me—"

Nemo stood up. "Thanks for the interesting consultation. I now see that I was never crazy to begin with. And don't worry about whether or not it was *our* Universe I named and awakened to consciousness. I could just as easily have invented an open sesame to unlock the door to another Universe, although I think it doesn't really matter. I can hardly wait to tell Stuffy that I don't have to go to Bellevue. I just have to get to work."

Stopping at the door, he smiled shyly. "Do you mind if I try to reproduce the sound again?"

"Well, no; but you still haven't told me what you remembered about the dream."

"Sure I did." Nemo wrapped his arms together over his chest, stood up straight, and seemed to let the mysterious word issue from his throat. It was not, I instantly realized, quite the same.

He looked at me, winked, and left.

"You've finished?" said the Oldest Member as the other Pshrinks hastily downed the dregs of their coffee and pushed aside the remains of dessert—Doughnuts Dysphagia.

"Not quite," said the Interpersonal, watching as the Pshrinks began to push back their chairs too.

The Oldest Member rapped a spoon sharply upon his water glass. "If there's more, I want to hear it. I am certain that the intrapsychic structure of—"

One of the other Interpersonals sighed and said, "Did Nemo end up in a hospital?"

"Yes," said the Oldest Member grudgingly, "what are the facts? Of course, in analyzing the case, it's obvious that the libidinal aberrations in the preschizophrenic dereistic thinking—"

"Nemo's not and never has been in a hospital," said the Interpersonal, picking up a doughnut. "I wonder if we too often examine the doughnut closely while forgetting to notice what's in the middle."

"Are you explaining or going into one of your Zen states?" asked one of the Eclectics.

"Sorry about that," said the Interpersonal. "You see, Nemo *did* tell me what he had suddenly remembered while sitting in my office. 'It was nothing,' he said. I think he meant it with a different emphasis, more like 'It was *Nothing.*' Not the doughnut but the hole."

"You aren't making any sense at all," said the O.M., pulling at one of his silver moustaches.

"That's what Nemo would undoubtedly say. He's doing fine, and is about to blast the world with the products of his years of research, according to an article I read in one of my husband's scientific journals. I think—I'm not positive—that he's concentrating on the doughnut."

The Oldest Member grabbed the other end of his moustache.

"Nemo's a fabulous success," said the Interpersonal hurriedly. "He's a millionaire already from his computer-science inventions and expertise. He's financed his own private research, which he says is about ready to be unveiled. I got a card from him last Christmas saying that I should take note of how useful his mysterious word was going to be."

"Bah!" said the O.M. "You expect us to believe that a noise he once dreamt could be useful without years of strict classical analysis?"

"Yes. Nemo's current work in artificial intelligence is on a machine apparently capable of speech, not only human sounds but also those no human throat can make. These robots have more than rudimentary thinking abilities, and their mental skills can develop as the artificial brain experiences life and, presumably, itself. I'd guess that Nemo expects the robots to be able to reproduce that name perfectly and thus leap faster into consciousness."

"But you said the word was a name that makes the whole Universe come alive," said a Jungian disconsolately.

"Oh, yes," said the Interpersonal airily, waving her hand as if to include and then dismiss the Universe, "but consider the other implications for all us little ripples in the fabric of the Universe. Suppose the name works because it tunes into nothingness—*any* nothingness—and gives it the urge to become somethingness?"

The Oldest Member abandoned the support of his moustaches and clutched at the unlit cigar that always lay within comforting view beside his plate.

"I suppose I should explain," said the Interpersonal, "although it's embarrassing."

The O.M. perked up. "There, there, m'dear. Be open. We hold everything in strictest confidence. What's a little neurosis among colleagues? Perhaps we can help you to insight."

"It's the possibility of instant insight that bothers me," said the Interpersonal, peering through the doughnut. "I don't mind pure nothingness so much. I'm not sure I want it *all* to turn into somethingness."

"She's off again," said one of her colleagues.

"I'd better tell you about Stuffy," said the Interpersonal contritely. "Shortly after my consultation with Nemo, Stuffy found himself another wife, suddenly shaped up as an analyst and graduated from analytic school, grew longer hair, wore interesting clothes, learned to cook exotic Chinese food, and went to another part of the country to found his own analytic institute."

"What's that got to do with Nemo's alien word, or with nothingness?" said the Oldest Member.

"I'm convinced that when Stuffy heard Nemo's word, he heard it to the core of himself, and it changed his life. I think the word names not only the Taoistic nothingness of the entire Universe of reality, but tunes into the nothingness of each person. Tunes into both what isn't there and what is potentially there."

"You mean . . ."

"Poor old Stuffy. Getting thoroughly in touch with one's own stuffy emptiness must have been a galvanizing experience. Nemo doesn't realize that happens because he doesn't recognize his own emptiness as anything terrible. He's a genius scientist, and to him emptiness is exciting—something from which form emerges, something which can be filled, and named."

"But how do you know?" said the Oldest Member.

"Unfortunately, I don't," said the Interpersonal, crumbling the doughnut. "I only know what it felt like when Nemo stood in my doorway and repeated the sound of the name. For an agonizing moment I knew exactly who and what I was and could be, bad and good. Being human, I immediately forgot, or repressed, everything but a vague impression, but that was enough to accelerate my own personal analysis."

"Then what are you worried about?" asked the O.M., tasting a doughnut crumb.

"Nemo's robots will pronounce the name perfectly. What will that do to us humans?"

"Make Pshrinks busier," said the O.M. complacently. "And there's no evidence that hearing the name definitely made you any less or more impossible than you always were."

The Interpersonal kissed him on his left moustache. "You ought to think about going into psychoanalysis for robots. I think you'd be good at it, and they may need it."

"Why?"

"If I read the information about Nemo correctly, those robots of his will be able to pronounce the word easily. They and they alone. And what happens when they become intelligent enough to get instant insight and start thinking about potentials to emerge from their own emptiness? Does the Universe deserve . . ."

"It certainly deserves everything it gets," said the O.M. "And now, in view of the interesting nature of this case presentation, I think we should vote on having Nemo as a luncheon speaker, bringing sound-producing equipment or even a robot or two . . ."

"What a great idea!" said the Interpersonal. "We could all get in touch with our own stuffiness!"

There was a frantic scramble as the other Pshrinks all headed for the exit.

THE TIME-WARP TRAUMA

In the hotel headquarters of a luncheon club called the Psychoanalytic Alliance, it was not immediately apparent that summer was arriving in Manhattan. The subbasement dining room was as dim as ever; the plastic flowers on the sideboard still as faded; the waiters no more languid than usual.

Nevertheless, a noticeable change could be detected in the demeanor of Pshrinks Anonymous. Clothing was lighter in weight and color. There were no briefcases bulging with unread journals as well as dog-eared manuscripts of theoretical papers in search of a publisher. The members talked about vacations instead of work, funny movies instead of psychological films, love instead of sex, and they smiled cheerfully. Some even quoted poetry.

All except the Oldest Member. He had arrived, for once, earlier than anyone else, but was strangely silent as the room filled up. His tweeds were rumpled, the waxed tips of his luxuriant white moustache drooped, and he sucked meditatively on an unlit cigar. The fact that his Salade Sullivan was untouched may have been due to his unreconstructed Freudianism, but other Pshrinks whispered that the O.M. was distinctly off his feed.

"Perhaps he's just come from having an EKG at his internist's," whispered a Pshrink, scratching his chest over his pacemaker.

"New York City bonds are probably down again," diagnosed a Pshrink who favored Ego Psychology as well as Swiss banks.

An Interpersonal looked at her watch and yawned. "I have lots of time," she said. "My first afternoon patient is away on vacation early, and I think I should give you all the benefit of some in-depth research I am doing on the sexual pleasures of the middle-aged, the intensity of which would give Freud pause, since it is quite probable that as he grew older . . ."

The Oldest Member did not seem to react.

"The moustaches are not rising to the bait," said another Interpersonal.

"Oh hell; it's too close to summer vacation to listen to

anything today," said an Eclectic. "It's bad enough having to sit in our offices and listen to tales of woe."

"You object to listening to your patients!" said several Pshrinks.

"Not exactly," said the Eclectic, "but right now my wife calls frequently to tell me her latest plans for an impossible vacation with all her relatives . . ."

"Spouses are off conversation limits," said the Interpersonal, who was well known to have unseemly passion for her own spouse.

The Oldest Member pursed his lips. Then he grunted.

Waiting silently, the other members of Pshrinks Anonymous shuffled their feet and glanced nervously at each other. The Oldest Member did not speak.

The Interpersonal reddened and said, "I'm sorry, spouses aren't exactly taboo topics—although I realize everyone is sick of hearing about mine—so I don't want to inhibit anyone else's conversation."

"Um," said the Oldest Member, sitting up straighter for a second. Then he slumped back.

"Before I have nervous prostration," said the Interpersonal anxiously, "please tell us what's the matter."

"Only a difficult case," said the Oldest Member truculently, "in fact, I could say a fascinating case, but you all seem so bored with our beloved profession, now that summer has started, so absorbed in your vacations that I am displeased with your lack of serious conversation about psychoanalytic issues."

Several Pshrinks hastily looked at their watches, fingered their vacation brochures, and made attempts to rise.

"Sit down!" roared the Oldest Member. "I will now describe the case which has been occupying my attention today. The patient was a man afflicted with that permanent vacation known as retirement. Not that he was absolutely required to retire at the age he did, but his spouse insisted, disregarding the fact that, as the world's population ages, the antiquated notion of mandatory retirement is rapidly undermining civilization, which should not lose the capabilities, the training, and knowledge of so-called senior citizens, most of whom are unhappy and frustrated over being cast aside."

"But—" said the Youngest Member.

"And furthermore, all of you should be grateful that ours is a fortunate profession, a remarkably long-lasting summertime of being in one's prime until there's nothing left but winter. Psychoanalytical expertise and acumen increase with the years, making retirement not only unnecessary but unwise."

"Hear! Hear!" said Pshrinks who were middle-aged and up.

"Naturally you agree with me. You will also appreciate the difficulties posed in working with this patient. Actually, his problem turned out to be so unusual that—but I am sure you find it impossible to imagine that there could be any mental conditions with which I have not had professional experience."

"Perish forbid," said the Interpersonal solemnly.

"Thank you," said the Oldest Member.

My patient [the O.M. explained], a Mr. Y, had an unusual form of altered state of consciousness in which he believed himself to have been transported bodily into another time and place. I have told you this to begin with because, unlike *some* members of this club, I do not believe in narrating a story in such a way as to arouse suspense. I give you the facts plus subsequent description and pertinent explication, as any Pshrink should do in presenting a case report to his fellow professionals.

Mr. Y was referred to me by one of my oldest colleagues, whose husband had also been forced into obligatory retirement and had insisted that my colleague move with him to one of those adult housing colonies—the kind that is surrounded by barbed wire and patrolled by attack canines at night—in one of the sun states, where Pshrinks betray the principles of analytic technique and lapse into neurotic acting-out from which they would have been safe in Manhattan, where we are not likely to hold marathon group sessions in communal hot tubs in the open air to investigate patterns and possibilities of genital and extragenital touching, to say nothing of phony emotional catharsis supposedly achieved by much yelling and baring of fangs at one's immediate neighbor and . . .

"I had a little trouble following that sentence," ventured one of the younger Pshrinks. "I'm also under the impression that you don't know what's going on in Manhattan . . ."

. . . and I don't *want* to know [said the Oldest Member]. At any rate, this patient—according to my colleague, who was, naturally, forced to give up her Manhattan practice—was very close to termination of his analysis; and I was to finish it. After our first interview, I believed that he would need merely a few months of integrating the excellent work already done, during which his various sexual problems had been analyzed satisfactorily, so that he was happy with his third wife and remembered his mother with insight.

Mr. Y was even older than his former analyst, but—as you know—we modern Pshrinks have discovered that the psychoanalytic technique of investigating the psyche is quite suitable for older patients. My retired colleague and I believed that Mr. Y was an analytic success and had adapted to the stress of retirement.

Mr. Y had a pension from his job plus accumulated capital, and had just inherited from his brother a small cooperative apartment on Central Park West, which he and his wife could well afford. He could even afford me, although I did not expect he would have to stay in treatment long. I resisted the temptation to make his analysis as perfect as possible, exploring and resolving the remaining oedipal problem now that at last he had a male analyst . . .

"There's always an unresolved residue of oedipal problem," said one of his more pedantic colleagues at the other end of the table.

"For Freudians," said the Interpersonal.

. . . but after we had worked together that winter and spring, we decided to terminate at the start of my vacation. That was last summer. Just a year ago. Little did I realize . . .

But first I must explain that Mr. Y, prior to moving to Manhattan in retirement, had always lived in the suburbs, from which he had commuted by train and then taxi to his job in the financial district. He worked in one of those solid establishments that looks like a refined fortress of classic style with heavy brass doors and the proper amount of metal grillwork to be closed by human hands when one takes the elevator. He had always felt safe at his job, and in Grand Central Station, which of course he never saw except at hours when it was full of other well-dressed people from the suburbs going to or coming from work . . .

"Considering that you don't believe in creating suspense," said a Pshrink steeped in the mysteries of Object Relations, "I wonder why it's killing me?"

"Ah," said the Oldest Member through the Buttered Borderline Bun he had savagely bitten into after being interrupted, "perhaps your restlessness has deep roots in your id."

The Interpersonal looked at the cobwebs on the ceiling. "You are, I think, telling a story fraught with clinically intriguing implications, but one wonders if you've ever had any traumatic experience with editors of psychoanalytic journals."

"They wouldn't dare," said the Oldest Member, brushing crumbs off his flamboyant tie. By now his moustache points were erect.

As I was saying [continued the Oldest Member firmly], Mr. Y began living on Central Park West at about the same time that he entered analysis with me. It was his first encounter with actual city living, and like most out-of-towners he was full of fears about the dangers in Manhattan.

There was a police lock on the door of his apartment, iron fencework over his windows; and he refused to go outside at night or in Central Park at any hour although, like myself, he was tall, physically robust, looked younger than his years, and walked with brisk assurance. He was therefore in little danger from muggers; but in spite of our analytic work on the subject, he did not choose to walk in the park.

Yet there, outside his windows, was Olmsted's magnificent creation, littered and looted and graffitied to be sure, but still worth experiencing. To get to my Fifth Avenue office he actually took taxis through the transverse street! One day he began to notice that, as summer's warmth came closer, the park seemed to be safely full of happy people of nonvillainous aspect. He began to contemplate the daring experiment of walking what amounts to only four long blocks from Central Park West (really Eighth Avenue) to my office on Fifth.

At the next-to-final scheduled session, Mr. Y announced that he felt so free of neurosis that he could enjoy not only retirement but the decision to walk through the park. "I am capable of being like everyone else," he said.

He had not wanted to be like everyone else to begin with. According to his previous analyst, he had resented his stodgy job; his inhibited first wife; his originally scandalous second wife, who upon marriage took up bridge and the Junior League; his conventional sons, who were duplicating his previous suburban existence; and his history of traveling only in group educational tours that were tax-deductible, safe, and boring.

Mr. Y had even been a surreptitious subscriber to a disreputable brand of literature known as science fiction, but after a few sessions with me the last shreds of attachment to it seemed to have cleared up. At least, he did not talk about it anymore.

I was pleased that he had decided to walk across the park to his last session. I felt that it was a suitable culmination to a successful analysis, and as an old—I mean *longtime* New Yorker, I did not in the least feel concerned about his plan. Therefore I was as shocked as any trained, self-respecting Pshrink is ever likely to be when Mr. Y came to his supposedly final session in a psychologically deteriorated state.

"I've just had a terrifying experience in the park," he said, flopping down on my couch. "I hope I'm just psychotic—something simple and normal like that. I don't think it could be a developing phobia about birds, although I did rather resent my older sister's attention to our parakeet."

I waited—I am a Freudian, you know—but he did not continue. He turned around so that he could look out my office window to the green of the park. It was already such a warm day that I was using the air conditioner. I decided that, due to the abnormal, unanalytic conditions of this last interview, I had better ask questions.

"What happened?"

"I think I sat down in a time warp. It was at the top of a hill where they're doing a lot of construction inside—the hill, that is, some subway extension—and the ground was vibrating. I sat down on a bench to rest for a minute and the machinery stopped. I noticed a bird on a nest in a nearby tree."

"It reminded you of your mother?"

"Hell no. It looked like a healthy, maternal, friendly creature; probably a robin. What happened was that the sun was so warm I felt sleepy. Perhaps I dozed. I don't know. I think the machinery started up again, and suddenly everything blurred. When it righted, the scene was different. The trees were not the same and I was sitting on a warm stone, not on a park bench."

"Have you ever before had dreams that seemed like reality?"

"Not like this one. I wish I'd thought to pick a leaf or something, to prove I was actually there."

"Where?"

"I don't know. I took biology in high school, but that was a long time ago. The robin looked like another bird, and Manhattan sounded odd. Usually there's a constant background noise, a sort of pulsating hum as if the city were breathing out there, but that was missing. I'd been sitting in a place where you couldn't see buildings for the trees, but when the bird changed, everything changed. It felt as if the city were gone."

"Tell me about the bird."

"Ugly creature, bigger than a robin. More like a crow, sitting on a limb near me. When I moved, it leapt up and soared down over my head, gliding into some tall bushes where it disappeared. For a minute I thought it was going to rake my head with the claws on its wings."

"Claws? Are you sure?"

"That's right. I hope I was dreaming, because the bird screamed as it went by and I could see that there were teeth in its beak. I didn't like the long, snaky tail either, for all that it had rather pretty purple feathers on it."

"I've always wanted to know what color archaeopteryx was," said the Interpersonal.

The patient calmed down on my couch—it often has that effect, especially since I put an old oriental rug on it to cover the worst holes. At first I thought the rug would be distracting, but then I remembered the photograph of the Master's cluttered office and . . . where was I? Ah yes. When I was questioning the patient, it occurred to me that no doubt he had seen a picture of the late Jurassic period and for some reason hallucinated it when he rested on the way to my office. I told him as much, and said that this sort of hypnagogic hallucination is common in the twilight zone between waking and sleep. Common and not dangerous.

"Can't you put off your vacation, Doc? I want another session."

"Very well. We will explore the psychodynamics of the content of this particular mental aberration, and perhaps find out what caused it."

"Besides senility?" asked Mr. Y with a feeble laugh.

"Nonsense—you and I are the same age," I blurted out, a mistake I have hardly made since those harrowing days of my own training analysis which caused me to overidentify with my own patients.

Mr. Y laughed heartily. "I'm glad you're human, Doc."

It was humiliating. I saw Mr. Y to the door, fully expecting that he would return for the next visit quite recovered from his fright. Unfortunately, I was so preoccupied by the fantasy of a time warp that I forgot to warn him not to walk through the park to his next visit, for we had to investigate his use of the maternal symbolism of birds, and the psychic trauma implicit in the emphasis on teeth and claws.

"A toothed beak isn't as fraught with portent as a vagina dentata, is it?" asked the Interpersonal.

I will not answer frivolous questions. This is a serious case presentation about the obscure restlessness that can afflict people who are forced to retire, to sit on benches in the warmth of sunlight, when memories and fantasies become more intense—[the Oldest Member paused and sipped his coffee. It was noted that his hand trembled slightly.]—so when Mr. Y returned the next time saying he was definitely psychotic, I was perturbed.

"This time I wasn't sleepy, I swear it," said Mr. Y. "I was walking along the same road in the park, congratulating myself that I was wide awake and in full possession of my senses—as indeed I have been since I saw you—and I stopped for just a moment to look at that same robin. She didn't change at all, and I walked on feeling pleasurably sane, remembering the old road near my small hometown where I used to walk with my first girl, when suddenly I felt hemmed in by the sight of buildings in the distance and wished I were in the country."

Mr. Y stopped, his eyes suspiciously moist. "It seems that all my life I've been secretly wishing I were somebody else, somewhere else, but until I retired I never wished to go back, just forward to something more exciting than whatever I was experiencing. Now that I'm not working, there doesn't seem anywhere to go except the past . . ."

"Balderdash," I said.

"What do *you* know? You work. You've got a future! You'd never be so trapped in a dull present that you'd feel my longing for youth and its dreams of future glory, or experience my traumas of age, a fevered, out-of-control dissolving of *now* and finding oneself in *then*. I don't even have control over where I'm going in the past!"

"Now surely you don't believe you actually went there?"

"Yes. I was at the top of the hill when the machinery started up again. I felt dizzy, and suddenly the road was only a track of ground where the grass had been destroyed by many feet. Manhattan was gone, and I was in some other place with lots of trees containing horrible big birds with bald heads, just waiting for something to die."

"Have you been worrying about your mortality?" I asked.

"Now don't get psychoanalytic on me! I went back in time—"

"It's my job to get psychoanalytic."

"Then analyze this. I stumbled around a big rock and almost fell into some sort of swamp with bones littered everywhere. To the right was a loud noise, and soon an elephant came running hell-bent for leather with a pack of wolves at his heels."

"I doubt if wolves and elephants cohabit the same ecology."

"They did then, whenever it was. They came closer, and I saw that the elephant was much bigger than any I'd ever seen, so big that the wolves ought to have seemed smaller, but they were big too. The elephant had enormous tusks curving around so the points of them were aimed at his own body. His skin was a pale gray, covered with old scars. Dammit, he looked ancient—old and beat-up and being hustled into permanent retirement by those wolves." Mr. Y shuddered.

"What happened?"

"The elephant and wolves—which were clinging by then to his trunk and tail and ears—stumbled straight into the swamp, which seemed terribly sticky. It trapped them. They couldn't get out. They bellowed and howled and floundered deeper and deeper . . ."

"Yes?"

"That elephant. I'm positive that it knew it was old; and it wanted to die there in the swamp, fighting its enemies. I watched until suddenly I knew that an enemy was watching *me*. I turned and to my left, up on a ledge just over my head, an enormous mountain lion with fangs crouched, aiming itself at me. It snarled through those fangs and leapt."

He seemed to have come to a full stop. "And?" I said.

"Then I was looking at a smaller green cat. It was a statue, perched crouching on a rock over the roadway in Central Park. I'd never seen it before."

"I know that statue well," I said. "It's a cougar, but I think you thought you saw a saber-toothed tiger. Have you been to

the Museum of Natural History, or seen reproductions of
Knight's pictures of the La Brea tar pits?"

"No."

"You probably have. The scenes of death and destruction
impressed themselves on your unconscious, and the cougar
statue, like the robin, triggered off another hypnagogic hallucination."

"But retirement is death for me! Maybe it would cure me
if I took a job. An old business pal of mine retired a couple of
years ago and sank his capital into an elegant midtown restaurant. He jokes with me about his problem of getting
dignified help. Right now he needs a maître d'—and I've
always wanted to be one."

"Um. Possibly your problems of ego gratification and
power needs should be analyzed. . . ."

"First I'll take the job. My wife will just have to adapt."

So he did, and she did, and we finished the analysis by the
next winter.

"I hope you analyzed the anal implications of those hypnagogic hallucinations," said a Freudian.

"I hope you noticed that Mr. Y is working himself forward
in evolution—first the Jurassic and then the Pleistocene,"
said the Interpersonal.

Odd you should remark on that [said the Oldest Member,
caressing his moustache], since Mr. Y called for an emergency appointment this morning. As it happened, I had
canceled all my regular appointments because my wife and
I intended to look at a house in the country, but my car's
transmission wouldn't work right when they brought it up
from our basement garage. I went back upstairs to tell my
wife and the telephone rang. My wife was somewhat peeved
when I naturally canceled the trip so I could see a needy
patient, rather than having the transmission fixed.

"Naturally," murmured several Pshrinks.

Mr. Y ran to my couch. "I'm hallucinating again and I thought I was cured! I love my job, I feel great, my wife enjoys our Sunday walk in the park, and there haven't been any time warps, until I walked into the park this morning. It's your fault, Doc. My unconscious must have gone to work as soon as I looked up at your building across the park. I started thinking about you and me in the same age group and bang, there I was in the past again!"

"It's not Sunday, so your wife wasn't with you?"

"No, it's such a beautiful day I went in by myself, on my way across to Fifth, where I get a bus for my restaurant. When I passed by Belvedere Castle there was a maiden dressed in medieval costume waving from a window, and I could hear a stringed instrument playing a plaintive song. The castle looked new, and the jester lounging in its doorway wore a belled, pointed hat and upcurled shoes. I ran to Fifth and called you from a street phone. Here I am—should I go to a hospital?"

I stood up from my chair. "We will go into the park."

"But it's 1000 A.D. there—unless I'll be moved up to the French and Indian Wars or maybe Napoleon . . ."

"We will investigate," I said. And we walked over to Belvedere Lake with its backdrop of rock outcropping on which is perched the miniature stone castle.

Mr. Y was right. There was a maiden in the tower and a jester in the doorway.

"Come now—folie à deux?" said a Pshrink.
"Folly of cinema, I suspect," said the Interpersonal.

You are correct. A camera crew was in the bushes filming the scene as part of this summer's Shakespeare festival, which, as you know, has been getting stranger every year.

Mr. Y, ecstatic, balanced his checkbook on a rock while he wrote out my fee for a full session, which he insisted he had had. Then he bounded off to Central Park West to tell his wife before he went on down to work. He acted like a young squirt in love with life.

It was a highly satisfactory ending to a difficult case. If any of you wish me to discuss the more Freudian aspects of the psychodynamics, I will be glad to explain in detail . . .

In a cloud of muttered apologies, the assembled Pshrinks rose as one and headed for the exit. All but the Interpersonal, who sat watching the Oldest Member moodily gather up the leftover Chocolate Cathected Cookies.

"If the case satisfied you, why the continued look of perturbation?" she said. "If you tell me what's wrong, I promise not to tell anyone in your camp or mine."

"I suppose I need catharsis," said the Oldest Member dejectedly. "I have outlived all my own Pshrinks, and I shudder to think what my Freudian friends would say about the time warp *I* found in Central Park today."

"Perhaps all of us go into the past on some level of consciousness under certain conditions, particularly when aggravated by intimations of mortality as symbolized in incipient retirement," said the Interpersonal in her best analytic tones.

He eyed her suspiciously. "Are you trying to be an intuitive smart-ass?"

"I can't help it," said the Interpersonal modestly.

"Then shut up and listen. What happened was that as Mr. Y started home to the west, I went east, intending to stop at my office before coming here for lunch. I sat down near King Jagiello's statue—the equestrian one at the east end of Belvedere Lake—because I needed to think and it was hot walking. I could feel the vibration of the construction, over the hill just in back of the statue, where that bronze cougar sits facing the road. . . ."

"I know."

"There I was, sitting in the sun like a senior citizen, brooding about getting the car fixed so my wife and I could examine that house—which I suppose will be better to retire to than one of the blasted retirement colonies, her first idea— when suddenly I heard a voice yelling at me."

"Whose?"

"His. Jagiello. I opened my eyes to see him galloping across an unknown plain toward me, his two swords raised over his head, looking ferocious."

"Ordinarily he's quite handsome. What did he say?"

" 'Death to aggressors! Get out of my territory or prepare to meet your doom!' "

"In English?"

"Polish with a heavy Lithuanian accent. Would you believe that I found myself shouting back, in a mixture of Polish and Yiddish, 'I belong here! God will get you for this!' "

"I believe it."

"Then Jagiello scowled down at me—somehow the huge horse had stopped, with knee pressure, I presume—and he cursed me with appalling flamboyancy, calling me a misbegotten product of miscegenation."

"No wonder," said the Interpersonal. "Since he was busy defeating the Teutonic knights at the battle of Tannenberg in 1410, he must have been furious at your language mixture. I suppose your family—"

"Was a mixture," said the Oldest Member. "My grandmother, now that I recall, had a strong Lithuanian accent. Perhaps my unresolved oedi—"

"Pooey," said the Interpersonal. "Just stay away from the park's statue of Alice and her Wonderland cohort until the construction vibration stops creating time warps. The real past is one thing, but the thought of falling down a literary rabbit hole rouses my incipient claustrophobia."

"My spouse ignores the claustrophobic aspects of retirement—which you are much too young to understand."

"*My* spouse keeps making noises about how I've been working as a Pshrink long enough!"

The Oldest Member patted the Interpersonal's shoulder. "Never mind. Let's go spit at King Jagiello on the way back to our offices."

"Okay. I'd like to risk time-warp trauma. Anyway, I firmly believe that archaeopteryx *was* purple."

"It's too late to find out," said the Oldest Member. "I think that both of us have decided to take my patient's recipe for cure. We're not going to retire."

The Interpersonal smiled.

ABOUT THE AUTHOR

J. O. JEPPSON is a practicing psychoanalyst, the author of five novels, and a short story writer whose work is familiar to readers of *Isaac Asimov's Science Fiction Magazine, Amazing Science Fiction Stories,* and *The Magazine of Fantasy and Science Fiction.* Her Pshrinks Anonymous stories, says Dr. Jeppson, are "fun to write because they combine my three great interests: science fiction, psychoanalysis, and Zen. Occasionally I even make passing, disguised references to my greatest interest, my husband"— who is Isaac Asimov. Dr. Jeppson lives in Manhattan.